Nyokabi

Torn Between Tradition and Rebellion, Volume 1

Wangui Turner

Published by Wangui Turner, 2024.

This is a work of fiction. Similarities to real people, places, or events are entirely coincidental.

NYOKABI

First edition. July 4, 2024.

Copyright © 2024 Wangui Turner.

ISBN: 979-8224823888

Written by Wangui Turner.

To my family

Prologue

Nyokabi closed her eyes, trying to conjure the image of her childhood home. But the years had blurred the details, leaving only a hazy yearning in her heart. She tried to reach deep into her memories hoping to hear her brother's voice in her head. A vision of her father's face came to mind. As it became clearer a look of worry and love with suppressed tears masked his pain. This was what he looked like when she waved goodbye the day she left for America.

She knew he was longing to see her as much as she longed to see him. She opened her eyes as she smelled her mother's cooking. "It can't be," she murmured as she looked around. She was still on the plane but could still smell the familiar aroma of a home-cooked meal. She turned around and noticed the flight attendants coming down the aisle with food. *Kenya Airways, serving Kenyan cuisine*, she concluded with a smile.

The passenger next to her was looking at her with concern. Nyokabi gave her an embarrassed smile. "Nothing. Just feeling nostalgic" she said as she put her tray down.

As she ate her meal, she thought about her brother who must be taller than her now. He was still a child when she left. She wondered if he still had the same energy and level of activity he had when she last saw him. Before she boarded the plane out of the United States, she had bought a toy car for him. Her brows narrowed. *He is a teenager now! Almost a man! That is not an appropriate gift for him!* she thought. She started biting the inside of her cheeks like she always did when she was nervous. She got up and walked to the bathroom. She did not need to go but she had a lot of nervous energy and needed a short walk. What if they don't like their presents? What if she did not fit in anymore?

I can't wait to see them but I am not sure who they are anymore, she thought. In the bathroom, she looked in the mirror and washed her face. She was thinking about all her life's milestones that her parents did not get to witness. She pulled a letter out of her pocket. It had a stain on it and it was creased in so many areas. She was delicate with it as she unfolded it.

Nyokabi,

I hope you are doing well. We miss you very much and would love to see your face one day soon.

Love,

Mom and Dad.

She read it again. It felt like every time she felt out of sorts, she reached for this letter for reassurance. A sense of calm washed over her. "I miss you too. I am on my way," she whispered as she put it back in her pocket. She walked back to her seat as the flight attendants were walking down the aisle gathering the meal trays. There were two hours left on the flight and she had to try and relax as much as she could.

She pulled the airplane blanket up to her neck and closed her eyes. She immersed herself in the memories of the warmth of the African sun caressing her skin, the sensation of vibrating energy that surrounded her as a child. The song, dance, and the drums made the ground vibrate under her bare feet. She had missed that familiar feeling of love from generations past. There was a palpable energy that embraced her. She smiled she knew that familiar feeling of home. As if the ancestors flew up to the sky to greet her and welcome her home.

She sighed wondering if Devon would be accepted by her family.

"Ladies and gentlemen, we are approaching Jomo Kenyatta international airport, and Kenya Airways welcomes you to Nairobi, Kenya, or better known to many as the capital of Kenya. The local time is 10 am and the temperature is 23 degrees Celsius. To all the passengers who are visiting, we hope you enjoy the beautiful, magical Kenya and to all the Kenyans and residents we say, "Karibuni Nyumbani" (welcome home). It was a pleasure having you on board! Thank you for flying with us."

"Mabibi na mabwana tunakaribia uwanja wa ndege wa Jomo Kenyatta na Shirika la ndege la Kenya la wa karibisha Nairobi. Kwa abiria wote wanaozuru, ni matumaini yetu ya kwamba mta pendezwa na nchi ya Kenya, na kwa wakenya wote, karibuni nyumbani. Kwa niaba ya ndege ya Kenya twa washukuru nyote kwa kuchagua kusafiri nasi, na twawatakia siku njema."

Nyokabi adjusted herself in her seat. She wondered who would be waiting for her at the airport. If no one was at the airport, she would be forced to figure things out by herself. She could always take a taxi but she knew things had changed so much since she was home. She was unsure if she would be able to find the way home with ease. She heard that the newly independent government had simply adopted the colonialist's constitution The thought of returning to an independent

Kenya was great but what did that mean for her family, which had been living in a land reserve.

She wondered if her family was still in the reserve getting food rations and being watched by home-guards. She clenched her fist and her brows creased. *Did the new government need to consult Britain on decisions? Was Kenya still paying taxes to Britain? How was that independence?*

"Are you OK? said the lady sitting next to her on the plane. "You look a little worried."

Nyokabi managed to give the lady a weak smile. She started biting the inside of her cheek again as she thought about Devon and who she had become.

"I am ok. I just haven't been home in a while." Nyokabi responded.

"Why do you look worried?"

"I am going to have to tell my family that I will be getting married soon. The man is not Kikuyu, he is African American."

"Oh! You must be nervous about what they will think about that."

"Among other things"

"Will it be a traditional wedding?"

"I still don't know. He and his family would not know what to do. I guess we have to figure that out."

"I am sure if they are willing to learn, someone will show them what to do."

The lady squeezed Nyokabi's hand which was still clenched. Nyokabi relaxed visibly and smiled.

Nyokabi looked out the window and for the first time in years, she could see her beautiful country. Everything was so green, save for the cracks that carried fresh clean water down the mountains and the picturesque waterfalls. She could have sworn she saw some animals moving on the ground even though at that altitude they would appear to be just dots on the ground. The intensity of the realization of how much she had missed home and all its beauty was overwhelming. Tears were flowing freely down her face and she did not make an effort to hide them.

Devon in Los Angeles CA.

Devon had been laying down for a while now, staring at the ceiling. His room was dark, but the usual peace was shattered by the garish blue and white lights filtering through his window. They pulsed like a mocking reminder of the chaos unfolding outside. A muffled yell pierced the night, "Stop resisting!"

Devon flinched, his grip tightening on a worn photograph that he was pulling from under his pillow. It was a picture of Nyokabi, her smile as bright as the intrusive lights, her eyes sparkling with warmth. However, she was a world away from the violence erupting outside.

Another yell, "What is going on?' It was a woman's voice laced with raw panic. Devon squeezed his eyes shut, the image of Nyokabi burning brighter in his mind. He could almost hear her infectious laugh, a sound that always chased away his worries. But here, in the face of this relentless violence, even the memory of her laughter felt fragile.

A knock on his bedroom door startled him. "Devon, are you in there?" It was his mom's voice, laced with concern.

"Yes Mom, same old shit going on out there."

"Okay, you better get some sleep and stop worrying about Nyokabi."

Devon knew his mom was trying to be reassuring, but sleep felt like a distant dream. He turned over several times, the image of Nyokabi refusing to be dislodged from his thoughts.

Gunshots rang out, shattering the fragile peace. Devon dove to the floor, a scream piercing the night air. Two more shots punctuated the scream, a horrifying symphony of violence.

"Why!? He did nothing. He was just sitting outside his house!" The woman's voice was raw with grief.

A hollow calm settled over Devon as the scene unfolded down the street. He didn't move, didn't look out the window.

"He tried to reach for my gun," the man who had been yelling commands spoke, his voice now calmer.

Another deep voice yelled back.

"You better get back." he continued in a condescending tone. "Don't come any closer."

Sirens wailed in the distance, a mournful counterpoint to the human drama playing out on the street.

Devon slowly got up and sat on his bed, his gaze fixed on the photo clutched in his hand. He didn't need to look outside to know what he'd see. The image of Nyokabi's vibrant smile felt like a cruel taunt in the face of this relentless reality.

"I think they just killed another black boy," Devon said, his voice barely a whisper.

His mother rushed into the room; her face etched with worry. She pulled him into a hug, her touch a small comfort in the face of the overwhelming fear.

"Did you hear that?" she asked. "Were those gunshots? Lord have mercy! Someone just lost a child!"

She pulled Devon a little closer protectively.

"I think Nyokabi is better off in Kenya," he said. "I don't want to marry her and have her in this environment."

Devon's mother rubbed his back, her voice soothing. "You love each other. You two will figure that out."

But even as she spoke, a seed of doubt had been planted. Devon loved Nyokabi, there was no question about that. But could his love protect her from this relentless violence? Was marrying her condemning her to a life of fear? The weight of these questions pressed down on him, a heavy burden amidst the chaos of the night.

Chapter 1

November 1949

The ringing of the bell marked the end of the lesson. Sister Madonna looked directly at Nyokabi, smiled, and signaled her to wait.

"We shall ride back to the convent together," Sister Madonna said with a smile.

Nyokabi knew there was more to that statement. Sister Madonna had a slight arch to her upper lip, a sign she was a little excited. Nyokabi had learned to read Sister Madonna's face. She had known her for several years now. She had moved into the convent and lived with several other nuns several kilometers from her home reserve where her family lived.

One night, the Mau-Mau had come through her reserve and had killed several people they believed had been conspiring with the home guards to give up their locations. Several home guards and several villagers had died in one night. Everyone was on edge and Nyokabi's mother had refused to allow her to walk to school alone. Sister Madonna negotiated on Nyokabi's behalf, enabling her to move to the convent. Sister Madonna had assumed the role of a mother and Nyokabi had no problem respecting her as such.

Nyokabi looked at Sister Madonna's face. She noticed that her once pale skin had started showing signs of sun exposure.

Her freckles were as dark as Nyokabi's skin. There were deep wrinkles that lined the sides of her mouth that deepened when she smiled. She also noticed a few grey hairs from the few that had escaped from under her veil. Her small petite body was beginning to look a little thinner. Nyokabi frowned wondering if sister Madonna was okay or if she was just getting a little older.

Sister Madonna was walking towards Nyokabi. She smiled lightly as sister Madonna approached her. She stared into her green eyes. She still had no idea how she could see with those green eyes. Sister Madonna touched Nyokabi's hand and squeezed it. A warmth swept over Nyokabi. She had grown to love this woman despite the sentiment towards "white people" in the country.

"How are you doing?" Sister Madonna asked.

"Okay," Nyokabi replied with a frown, wondering where the conversation was going.

"You have not visited your family for several weeks and I was wondering if you would like to go see them tonight." Sister Madonna said with a big smile. "I have also been craving some of your mom's yams."

Nyokabi was excited about the prospect of seeing her parents and her brother. "Can we?"

"Absolutely!" Sister Madonna said. "I have an important matter I would like to talk to your father about as well."

Nyokabi grabbed her books and some fell to the floor as she hurried to stuff them in her backpack. Sister Madonna helped her pick them up. She was trying not to laugh. She loved Nyokabi and always wanted to see her happy.

Nyokabi's smile faded and a frown replaced the smile. She wondered why they had to go to the reserve on a weekday and this late in the afternoon. She worried about their safety on the trip there and back.

Sister Madonna had known Nyokabi since she was a child. During this time, she had grown to love Nyokabi as if she was her own. Nyokabi had stood out as a stellar student from the very first day she came to the secondary school. She had big bright eyes and an insatiable hunger for learning new things. Sister Madonna straightened her sweater as she looked at Nyokabi. Her body was changing and her curves were beginning to show. Her waist was receding, there was a slight outline of breasts on her white blouse, her facial features were taking shape too and her high cheekbones were visible now that the baby fat was melting away. She was turning into a beautiful young woman.

"Let's drop your books off at the convent and then go see your parents. Sister Madonna said. "I will meet you at the van. I have some important papers to pick up."

Sister Madonna watched as Nyokabi walked away. Nyokabi walked with a confidence that exuded grace and self-respect. Boys would look at her as she walked by as if they were hypnotized by an unseen force. Despite this attention, she remained humble which made her even more pleasant to be around. Nyokabi had noticed the way some boys looked at her. Their gazes lingered a little longer than usual which made her uncomfortable. She did not know how to respond to them or how to get them to stop.

The girls, on the other hand, would look at her as she walked by—some with a flicker of admiration, others with a hint of disapproval. A slight frown creased Nyokabi's brow as she caught a whisper about marriage from a group of younger girls.

She was the only girl in her class her age. Most other girls had dropped out and were already married. As she walked, a familiar wave of uncertainty washed over her. She glanced down at her books, then back up at the path ahead. Schooling offered a future unlike any she knew, a future filled with knowledge and possibilities. Yet, tradition loomed large.

This trip back home felt different this time. Sister Madonna's cryptic comment about her father, the weight of unspoken expectations, and the danger of the Mau-Mau all swirled together in Nyokabi's mind. She knew this visit would likely bring a conversation about her future, a conversation that could change everything.

Chapter 2

Nyokabi quickly changed out of her school uniform and into a circular blue skirt and white blouse. They had been donations but they fit her perfectly. She walked out of the convent to find sister Madonna waiting for her by a van.

"Are we bringing the usual escorts for protection? Nyokabi asked Sister Madonna. "The Mau-Mau are going after the settlers. I would not want you to be targeted."

"Oh, don't worry about me Nyokabi," she said. "A convoy is scheduled to be bringing supplies for the home guards at several camps including the one where your parents live this evening and they will be right behind us."

"Oh okay. So we will be waiting for them, then?"

"According to our plan, they should be driving by in five minutes," Sister Madonna said looking at the watch she had pulled out of her pocket. It was a silver watch with a silver chain that was tethered to something in her pocket. Nyokabi had never found out how she kept it from falling. She had seen it dangling out of the pocket without falling but sister Madonna managed to put it back in the pocket most of the time.

"Oh no!" Nyokabi exclaimed. "I am so sorry I should have hurried."

"It is okay. We can make it if we leave right now."

The fear washed over Nyokabi's face again. She did not like that they were going to be on the road on the way back after sunset. She walked to the jeep. They drove out of the convent onto the road and a distant roar of engines became audible. Before long, they saw the home-guard convoy. Which rolled to a stop near them.

Sister Madonna walked over to the first jeep and was talking to someone. Nyokabi looked back to see the home guard's khaki uniform, which looked like it was made out of thin wood. Each of them carried a gun on their back that seemed to be trying to pierce the sky. They had an emotionless blank stare and that was frightening to Nyokabi.

Nyokabi could not help but have some contempt toward them. These were Africans doing the colonialist's bidding. She faced forward and fixed her gaze on the road. This was the only road that came from Nairobi and it split into different tributaries to different camps where her people had been relocated by the colonialists.

This land had been theirs for eons until the British came and decided they wanted the most fertile land. Rounded up the occupants, drew imaginary lines, called them borders, and divided them amongst themselves. They had rounded all the rightful owners, placed them all in different camps, and fed them rationed food. They even went a step further and placed a curfew on them and enforced movement. For someone to move from their camp, they needed a pass showing that they had been granted permission to do so.

Most Africans did not know a lot about these rules or their origins. She had access to a library and could read all the books except some that were "forbidden" according to Sister

Margaret. Nyokabi had tried to abide by that rule but her curiosity had gotten the best of her one day. She had smuggled one of the books to her room.

Nyokabi's almost photographic memory was sometimes a curse as she could remember almost everything she read. She closed her eyes tight. She was trying to forget the words in that first article that lit a fire in her. She did not know this new feeling she was having or what to do with it. As she closed her eyes tighter and her fist bawled in a tight fist, she could see the words clearly. It was handwritten as if someone was writing a research paper.

"The native reserves were established primarily under the guise that the Europeans felt it would be better for the native leaders to have more control over the natives if they were confined. However, it was more because the white settlers wanted the best land for grazing and farming. The Africans naturally felt that since they had prior claims to most land, there ought to be some reserves for whites rather than blacks.

"Their pushback was not very successful because the British military expeditions founded posts and imposed British rule in an increasing area by killing hundreds of Africans who opposed them. Thus in 1906 reserves were set up for the Kikuyu, Akamba, and many other communities. The Africans did not have any rights defined. The men were forced to leave the reserves to look for employment as they still had to pay taxes or lose all that they had to the government of the day. Most of the Africans in the reserves were therefore women and children.

"Back in Europe, the stereotypes of the "dark continent" and the numerous colonial allusions to imperial heroes were embraced. Soldiers who ventured into Africa were frequently

depicted as dauntless figures in conflict with savages or rebels. Such images helped to justify the European military, political, and missionary presence in the colonies."

The article went into detail justifying why the Africans needed an education because some would be useful in low-skilled positions and the ones who were not smart enough to learn a skill would be useful in manual labor. Nyokabi knew that the settlers had been having trouble getting the people to work on their farms, which was not surprising. For heaven's sake, they were asking the Africans to work as laborers in their own land growing food that was not helping their families like coffee, and sisal!

Nyokabi closed her eyes tighter. Her hand bawled in a tight fist, and her skin stretched and started to shine. She could see the words clearly in her mind, the stark truth about the land seizures and the justifications used by the colonizers. A new feeling burned within her; a simmering anger mixed with a strange sense of purpose. It was a feeling she didn't quite understand, but it demanded an outlet.

As she squeezed her eyes shut, a fleeting thought crossed her mind. Perhaps, the knowledge she gained wasn't just for her own personal growth. Maybe, it could be a weapon—a tool to fight for justice, for her people, for the land that was rightfully theirs.

Sister Madonna walked back into the van and closed the door. "Okay", Sister Madonna said. "They will be happy to escort us back but we should be ready to meet them at an agreed area on the drive back when they are done with the other camps. Which means we only have an hour with your family."

"I am sorry," Nyokabi said, forcing herself to focus on the present. "What did you say? We have one hour?"

"Yes, that should be enough if we hurry," Sister Madonna said.

Even as she responded, Nyokabi couldn't shake the feeling that this stolen knowledge, this newfound awareness, had ignited a spark within her. The hour with her family would be precious, but a seed had been sown. The question now was, how would she choose to use the knowledge that burned so intensely within her?

Chapter 3

After a brief period of silent driving, Sister Madonna took a deep breath in and stole a glance at Nyokabi who seemed to be so far away.

"How would you like to join an advanced-level high school next year, Nyokabi? You did very well and Sister Maria accepted my proposal to admit you next year," Sister Madonna said with a smile.

Sister Madonna's voice penetrated her thoughts, bringing her back to the scary drive through the war zone that was once her peaceful home.

Nyokabi had thought about this regularly. She would be the first girl in her home or even the reserve to join an A-level high school. Her father had seven wives and he wanted all his fifteen children to get an education. Most of the boys had gone to high school, one had even gone to Makerere University, but all the girls had been married off right after dropping out of high school. What would that mean for her, and what were her family's expectations of her?

Her mom would be happy, but she wasn't sure about her stepmothers. If it was all up to her, she would continue with her education. Of course, she wanted to go, but she dared not say anything yet.

The only one whose opinion truly mattered was her dad, so all she needed was his consent and the decision would be final. She figured that's why they needed to make this trip. Sister Madonna had to get consent from Nyokabi's father, and the only way to do so was to speak to him in person. Nevertheless, Nyokabi wondered why the conversation couldn't wait.

"I was just thinking about it this afternoon," Nyokabi said. "I think I would like to continue with my education if I can."

"I had a feeling you would say that," Sister Madonna said with a smile.

Nyokabi smiled back, but a strange sensation prickled at her skin. Sister Madonna's enthusiasm was genuine, but a tiny voice in Nyokabi's head whispered, *"Project...You are her project."* She pushed the thought down. Sister Madonna had been like a second mother to her. Why would she question her intentions now?

"I want you to know that even though you'll be in a different school, you can always come to me for help anytime if you need anything," Sister Madonna said with warmth. "Sister Maria is a wonderful person, and I'm sure the two of you will get along just fine. I will see if the mission will be able to get some money for your uniform and books. Everything will be paid for by the mission. You hear me? I don't want you to worry about anything."

Nyokabi mumbled a thanks, the prickling on her skin intensifying. It almost felt like Sister Madonna was talking about an object, not a person. The thought startled her. She had never had a negative thought towards Sister Madonna or questioned her motives before.

Nyokabi knew this was the only way to get her uniform and books. Her family had no money or any other means of procuring these items. The realization surprised her because deep down, a tiny seed of resentment bloomed. She loved Sister Madonna, but this strange possessiveness, this talk of "the mission" paying, made her feel like a charity case.

Her sisters would be even more envious of her once they found out. It was bad enough that she lived in the convent, this was going to widen the chasm between them.

"How do I deal with my sisters? They're always picking on me, saying Dad favors me more than any of his daughters," Nyokabi blurted out, surprised by the words leaving her lips.

"Don't worry, Nyokabi," Sister Madonna reassured her, her voice returning to its usual gentle cadence. "A time will come when your sisters will understand you, and things will fall into place then."

Nyokabi clenched her fists in her lap, the image of her sisters' sneering faces flashing in her mind. A time when they'd understand? They were already worlds apart. Here she was, about to embark on a journey to a completely different world, a world of high school and Sister Maria, whoever that was. She felt a pang of loneliness, a sense of being adrift between two worlds, no longer fully belonging to her family or the convent. Yet, despite the uncertainty, a flicker of determination ignited within her. Education was the only way forward, the only path to understanding the world that was fracturing around her, and the only weapon she had to carve out her own identity.

Chapter 4

The sun's rays were growing weaker under the canopy of the trees in the forest. Nyokabi looked around to see the security detail behind them and was more alert now. They were brandishing guns and being very diligent. The Mau Mau were known for their surprise attacks. The only noises she could hear were birds chirping as they were getting ready to settle in for the night, the rustle of leaves as the evening breeze swept over the trees and the sounds of vehicle engines.

They passed several other camps, and it always bothered Nyokabi that her people had to be kept in these gruesome camps. These were nothing like the villages her people lived in before. Here, huts were built close together with barbed wire surrounding the entire camp. The armed guards just made it worse by making the camps look like prisons. It was obvious it was an attempt by the government to flush out the Mau Mau and to make sure they didn't get any help from the people. At the same time, these conditions dehumanized her people and broke their spirits. She had this knowledge and anger, but no way of articulating it or fully understanding her predicament and that of her people.

Eventually, the camp that her parents lived in came into view, and she wondered what her dad would think once he saw the cars coming toward what he now called home. She saw her little brother running towards the path, and a smile tugged at her lips despite the knot of tension forming in her stomach. Mburu. She loved him so much, and he knew it. He was just three years old and the most adorable thing on the planet. As usual, there was the glum that always surrounded the people in the camps. Most men had a look of despair, most likely remembering the days they were important people in society.

Mama Njuguna, their neighbor, was sitting outside her hut with two other women. Her husband was nowhere to be seen. Nyokabi and Njuguna's families had been neighbors before they were moved to these hideous camps they called reserves. He had been very rich and respected in their village. Githinji, Njuguna's brother, was walking towards them. If things had been different, they would probably have been practicing Ngweko together. Who knows they probably would have been courting now. A smile started to form on her face, but something about him was different. He just looked at her with an intensity that sent shivers down her spine, like he could see right through to her soul. Then he looked at Sister Madonna, and Nyokabi could have sworn there was murder written all over his face. He walked right past them without as much as a greeting.

"Isn't that Njuguna's brother Githinji?" Sister Madonna said, her voice barely a whisper.

"Yes, sister," Nyokabi said. "He sure is acting strange today."

"Nyokabi!" Mburu called out, his tiny legs pumping as he ran towards her.

Nyokabi lifted him and cuddled him, the warmth of his small body was comforting amid the growing unease. "Where is mom and dad, Mburu?"

"Mom went to the farm with the home guards this morning, and dad is in Mama Njuguna's hut," Mburu said.

"Why?"

"Baba Njuguna killed himself this morning," Mburu said, oblivious to the bombshell he had just dropped.

Nyokabi's breath hitched. What? The world spun around her. Suicide? Here? Someone she knew? It was unthinkable. Grief stabbed at her, sharp and sudden, but underneath it all, cold anger simmered. This wasn't right. This wasn't fair. But how could she fight it? She was just a girl trapped between the confines of the convent and the despairing reality of her people. Tears welled up in her eyes, blurring her vision.

"Nyokabi!" Mburu tugged at her sleeve, his brow furrowed in concern. She forced a small smile for him, wiping her tears hastily. She couldn't break down now. Not in front of Mburu.

She put him down and started running towards Mama Njuguna's hut, her legs pumping with a newfound urgency. She had to get to her father to understand what had happened, what had driven Baba Njuguna to this drastic end.

Nyokabi fell right at Mama Njuguna's feet and started to weep. Mama Njuguna touched her, lifted her face, and said, "This is what they have reduced our people to. They have taken our best land and made it their own. They force us to pay taxes so we can work for them for nothing. Now my husband is dead because they were going to take what is left of his freedom away and because he doesn't have anything else left to give. They have taken everything including his life. At least, he left this world on his own terms. They think they are gods! Njuguna will see to it that his father's life is avenged!"

She looked up and saw Sister Madonna. "How dare you come here? Did you come to laugh at us? Did you come to see how we act when our people die?" She stood up and started walking towards Sister Madonna, but the home guards blocked her way and cocked their guns.

"No!" Nyokabi screamed. She was crying. Something she had gotten used to now. She was not ashamed of people seeing her tears anymore.

Nyokabi's dad walked out of the hut together with the chief and Njuguna's uncle. The chief still commanded some respect as far as Nyokabi knew. "Mama Njuguna, we don't want any more blood spilt," the chief said. "You should learn how to control your anger."

"But why?" Nyokabi thought.

"It only brings more harm than good," the chief continued, all the while staring at the home guards who had their guns pointed at them. Mama Njuguna who was taller than Sister Madonna, was still glaring at her. You could almost see her working through that anger in those few minutes, and her breathing slowed down enough for her to slowly start turning around.

"Sister Madonna, what brings you to these parts at this hour?" the chief asked Sister Madonna as he led her out of Mama Njuguna's hut.

Chief Wanjohi was a descendant of the Chief Wanjohi who had been murdered by the British when he resisted the building of the railroad through Kikuyu land. He had been buried alive and a lot was done to cover up the act. The story had been passed down nonetheless.

"I came to speak with Nyokabi's dad," Sister Madonna said. "There is some important news about Nyokabi I need to share with him."

"Very well, come to my hut so we can discuss this," said Nyokabi's father as he started to walk towards his hut.

Normally, when someone died, almost everyone in the village would go and comfort the family. In this case, people were not allowed to converge. The colonialists were paranoid and considered every meeting a venue to discuss "terrorism." Nyokabi felt sorry that no one would comfort Njuguna's family. Everyone had some sort of problem anyway and no one could console the other.

They walked into the hut and Nyokabi's dad took his usual seat. He still commanded respect from members of his family and they still respected him.

"I wanted to share some news about Nyokabi—" Sister Madonna started.

Chief Wanjohi cleared his voice and Nyokabi's father gave a short nod. Chief Wanjohi felt he had no reason to stay. He excused himself, bid them farewell, and left. Nyokabi sat on the floor next to her father. Mburu got a stool for his sister to sit on and he sat next to Nyokabi on the floor.

Chapter 5

"It is a pity we missed Nyokabi's mother," Sister Madonna said, trying to lighten the mood and set the stage for her news. "I would have liked to taste some of her yams."

The joke fell flat. Nyokabi almost felt embarrassed for Sister Madonna. Her face was almost the color of the volcanic soil that she knew so well. She must have been very uncomfortable.

Most Africans thought of the missionaries as friends who wanted peace because they provided education and treated their sick at the hospitals. However, at that point, the sister was the only white lady deep in the camp and she felt vulnerable although she didn't show it. Nyokabi was starting to feel like people identified her with the whites because she lived at the convent.

Most Kikuyu girls had been expelled from school because they had refused to give up their custom of female circumcision. Nyokabi could not help wondering what that had to do with their education but she had no one to ask. When the decision was made for Nyokabi to stay at the convent, it was on condition that Nyokabi did not get circumcised. Nyokabi's dad intended to have her at home for two weeks to go through this line of passage. Like every other girl her age including her sisters but with her being gone, that would be difficult.

Nyokabi's father reluctantly decided to wait till Nyokabi had completed her education. Living in the convent did not protect Nyokabi against the ridicule and scorn of the other girls who felt they were better than her because they had already been circumcised. She was considered a child because she was not circumcised. She would have been circumcised last year together with the other girls her age. If they were still able to practice their traditions, most of those boys and girls would have been getting ready for their Ngweko which was the event to find a husband or wife.

"Sister, just relax and tell me what brought you here today," Baba Nyokabi said. "I don't mean to be rude but I would like for you to get going before it gets dark."

Sister Madonna said: "I wanted to inform you that Nyokabi has been doing very well in school. I took the liberty of asking Sister Maria to admit her to an advanced-level high school and after she looked at her results, she was impressed enough to allow her to start in a few months. I will try to find some more funds from the mission to support Nyokabi's A-Level expenses. Nyokabi is happy to go and I really think she has the potential to go further than that."

Nyokabi's dad appeared to be in deep thought. Finally, with a smile, he said, "I will have to act as a referee when the other women pick fights with Nyokabi's mother but I am sure we will survive."

"It's settled then, Sister Madonna said. "We will come back and keep you informed."

Nyokabi couldn't understand her father's response until her mother walked in with a frightened look on her face. She looked at Nyokabi, managed a small smile, and then looked at the home guards. All expression left her face, and Nyokabi knew what she had to say could not be said in front of them. Her mother hugged her, Nyokabi clinging to her for a moment too long. Her eyes met with Sister Madonna and she smiled at her, but her eyes were anguished. She said, "You know girls her age are being abducted by the Mau Mau and people like you.... well...white people..."

"I know Mama Nyokabi," said Sister Madonna. "We were just about to leave. We have armed escorts so we will be safe."

"All the same I think it has become too dangerous to move about day or night, police escort or not," Mama Nyokabi said with a serious look on her face.

As they started to walk out of the hut, Mama Nyokabi pulled Nyokabi to a corner. A cold dread snaked its way down Nyokabi's spine as her mother began to whisper. One of the home guards saw it and started towards them, but Sister Madonna put her hand up to stop them. Nyokabi had never seen her mother like this. She stole a glance at her father. He did not react to this version of her mother. He must have guessed what was going on, or he had seen this side of her mother before today because he was not surprised. Her usually quiet and friendly mother was completely different today.

"I was pulled away by members of the Mau Mau today," her mother whispered, her voice trembling slightly. "I saw them today on our farm. The police were there but they cannot possibly see everything that is going on. They know where you are and they described you very well. They said I have to be taking food to a spot near the river and leave it there every day. If not, they would come and kill you."

Nyokabi's breath hitched. The Mau Mau? Targeting her? A whirlwind of emotions swirled inside her: fear, confusion, and a crushing guilt so heavy it threatened to suffocate her. Nyokabi was confused. The Mau Mau were supposed to be fighting for freedom, so why would they threaten her life?

"Mom," she whispered back. "I thought that the Mau Mau are on our side and that they are fighting for our freedom. Why would they do this?"

"Our people are in these camps so that we do not support the Mau Mau with food and weapons. We are guarded when we leave these camps. They say it is to protect us but the truth is, they don't want the Mau Mau sympathizers to help them in any way. I would do it anyway because I like what they are doing but now just taking the food to them will be risking my life. I would rather risk my life so you can live. We have a lot of hope in you."

"Mom, I would never forgive myself if anything happened to you because of me."

"Hush, child, and listen to me. I want you to promise that if anything happens to me, you will go on and study and make a difference for our people so my death is not in vain. I want you to take care of your brother and make sure he knows what happened."

"Mama don't say that."

"Nyokabi, listen to me. The way things are, this may be the last time I see you, although I pray it isn't so. Now is the only time, I can tell you this."

Nyokabi tried hard not to cry. She looked at the home guards and tried to conceal her emotions. "I promise, I promise I will work hard and make a difference."

"Now go before it gets too late," her mother said nudging her along.

Devon, Los Angeles CA 1949

Devon sat outside the front door with his friend Richard, their eyes glued to a picture of Jackie Robinson, the baseball legend. A sliver of admiration, sharp and sudden, pierced through Devon's heart. He had just won the International MVP award.

"I want to play baseball one day and be as famous as him," Richard declared, pointing at the picture. "My daddy said if I finish my homework early, I can go and practice and he will help me learn how to play."

Devon's gaze remained fixed on Robinson's picture, but a distant look clouded his eyes. He slowly looked down. "I don't think I could do it," he mumbled, the words heavy on his tongue.

"Do what?" Richard asked, tilting his head.

"I couldn't take all the racial slurs and dehumanization that he endures," Devon confessed, his voice barely a whisper.

A lump formed in his throat, the weight of unspoken dreams and unspoken fears threatening to choke him. He admired Jackie Robinson, no question about it. But the thought of what it took to face the relentless prejudice, the constant barrage of insults, just for a chance to play the game and win awards—that bothered Devon to his core.

Devon's mom opened the door. The smell of some home-cooked steak flooded the boys' nostrils. A familiar pang of guilt shot through Devon. He knew his mom had been stretching the groceries lately, forgoing extras like new shoes for him to make ends meet. "Hey, Richard! How are you?"

"I am fine Ms. Johnson. How is your mama? I haven't seen her in days."

"She is okay. She has been going to the hospital to see Uncle Harry."

"Why? What's wrong with him?"

"He was walking home last week and was stopped by the police. They asked him where he was going but didn't give him time to speak. They started beating him up and arrested him. I heard Mom saying that he is handcuffed to his hospital bed."

"Oh no!" said Devon. "Why didn't she tell me? Is she home?"

"I don't know I haven't been home since we left school," she said. "Richard, would you like to stay for dinner? I have plenty."

Devon narrowed his eyes, a suspicion flickering across his mind. He could have sworn his mom was wondering how to stretch the money they had until his dad's next paycheck.

Richard said, "I would love that Ms. Johnson, thank you."

Devon and Richard got up and walked into the house.

"Go wash your hands. Your dad will soon be home, Devon."

Devon's mom walked into the kitchen. After a few minutes, Devon smelled some eggs and smiled. She must be making some eggs to stretch the steak for Richard, he thought. A knot of frustration tightened in his stomach. He loved school, but dreams felt distant luxuries these days. How could he even think about college when his family was struggling to make ends meet? He hoped that his meeting with Ms. Wilson would work out.

"Well, Hello there beautiful!" Ray, Devon's dad, boomed as he walked into the house. Devon's mom was laying a bowl of mashed potatoes on the dining room table.

"Hey, baby. How was your day?" she responded. Ray walked over to his wife and kissed her on the cheek.

"Better, now that I am home." They both laughed and Ray took off his jacket and walked into their bedroom. Although he worked as an elevator operator, he wore a suit to work every day, changed into his uniform at work, and then back into his suit to go back home. Devon had never understood why he did that, but he knew most people around the neighborhood respected him. Devon and Richard had walked back into the living room after washing their hands. Richard had walked over to the seat closest to the dining room while Devon was in the kitchen helping his mother set up for dinner. Ray was already sitting at the dining room table.

Ray said, "Hey, Richard! How are you doing today? Did you already submit your application for college?"

Richard hesitated and shuffled his feet nervously, avoiding eye contact. A silent battle raged within him—the responsibility to help his family financially versus the burning desire to pursue his education like his friend Devon. He wasn't ready to voice this inner turmoil. "Well, Mr. Johnson, my uncle is in some legal trouble and we will need a lot of money to pay for a lawyer."

"Ray," said his wife. "Richard just told me his uncle is in a hospital handcuffed to his bed after the police beat him up."

Ray lowered his eyes and started shaking his head. "I don't know how long we will have to deal with this brutality."

Richard remained quiet, rubbing his right thumb with his left in a soothing gesture. Devon knew this conversation was making him uncomfortable, stirring up feelings of anger and helplessness.

"Hey, Dad! I just got the news that my college application was accepted and tomorrow Ms. Wilson will be helping me apply for the United Negro College Fund."

"That is good news, son," Ray said with a smile, a flicker of pride in his eyes.

"I know you are trying to change the subject, but I think police brutality and our constant fear is something that we should talk about," Devon's mother added.

"Or do something about," Devon chimed in. "I want to be able to represent people like Richard's uncle in court when I am done with college."

Richard looked at Devon, a crooked smile playing on his lips. "The way you argue with everyone about civil rights, you will make a great lawyer someday," he said.

"Okay, let's say grace so we can eat before the food gets cold," Ray said. Before closing his eyes to say grace, Devon noticed that his mom had added some egg sandwiches to the meal. She was always making sure everyone in her house was well fed even though they didn't have much.

Fort Hall, Kenya 1950
Chapter 6

Sister Madonna took Nyokabi's hand and they started to walk back to the jeep. Mburu started to cry, a sound that ripped through Nyokabi's heart. She was still struggling to process her mother's shocking revelation. A part of her yearned to stay to comfort her little brother and to play with possible future siblings. But another voice, quieter but insistent, reminded her of the opportunity for education, a chance to break free from the cycle of poverty and violence.

Nyokabi felt trapped between two worlds—a traitor to her family for leaving, yet harboring a secret hope for a better future. She climbed into the jeep, her head hanging low, tears finally spilling down her cheeks. Githinji stood a few meters away, his gaze fixed on her. This time, the message in his eyes was clear: *contempt*. Nyokabi understood.

They drove off into the evening. As the familiar landscape faded into the distance, Nyokabi noticed a crumpled piece of paper clutched in her palm. Her mother had slipped it into her hand just before saying goodbye. Curiosity battled with apprehension. What message did the note hold? Was it a final plea to stay, or a secret instruction that would further complicate her loyalties?

Nyokabi stole a glance at Sister Madonna, her face etched with understanding but a respectful silence. She knew better than to ask about the note, not yet. The weight of her mother's words and the hidden message in her hand added another layer of burden to Nyokabi's already heavy heart

As they got into town, A few kilometers from her parent's camp, Nyokabi was surprised to see Sister Madonna stop by Mama Wangui's store to buy a few supplies.

"I know we have to hurry but I want to promote Mama Wangui's business," she said.

Nyokabi stole a glance at the home guards. They only had a few guards with them. The rest of the convoy would meet up with them down the road. She saw a quick flicker of anger in the one who seemed to be in charge, which he quickly covered. They stopped their vehicle behind the jeep but they did not attempt to follow.

Mama Wangui was lifting empty sugar sacks from what looked like a pile of grain. Wangui, Wanjiru, and their other sisters crawled out from under the sacks. Nyokabi smiled in amusement.

"What game are you playing?" she asked.

Wangui and her sisters looked frightened. "Are you okay?" Nyokabi said. "What is going on?"

Mama Wangui who was staring at the home guards pulled Sister Madonna into the store. "What can I get for you today?" Sister Madonna pulled a list out of her pocket and the two ladies walked away to get those items.

Wangui frowned and watched her mother with a mixture of confusion and concern. Her mother had a big smile on her face as if everything was okay, which only made Wangui more uneasy. She and her sisters started dusting flour off their hair, faces, and clothes, a silent testament to their recent hiding place. Nyokabi felt a knot of confusion tighten in her stomach. What was happening?

Wangui leaned in and whispered in Kikuyu, explaining that the Mau Mau had been there about fifteen minutes ago, demanding food. "Mom is always afraid they will take us hostage," Wangui said, "so she hides us under the sacks whenever she hears they're coming."

Wangui paused and continued. "Today, the Mau Mau were here asking questions. They wanted to know if Mom had seen a convoy of home guards go by here earlier, and how long ago the convoy had passed. Also, where it was going and how many people were on it."

A chill ran down Nyokabi's spine. "What did she say?"

Wangui squeezed her hand reassuringly. "Don't worry, she said she hadn't seen a convoy because she was in the back. They didn't seem to believe her, and at some point, I feared for her safety. They took the food she had prepared for them and left."

"There must be someone informing them about the movements of people around here," Wanjiru said.

"You know, we were just at the camp and Mom was telling me–" Nyokabi started to respond in Kikuyu when she was cut off by a booming voice.

"Did you just say the Mau Mau? Were they here? What happened?"

The girls jumped, startled by the home guard standing right behind them. He hadn't been there a moment ago. Nyokabi's heart hammered against her ribs. He directed his gaze towards Mama Wangui, who glared at him with defiance.

Almost through gritted teeth, Mama Wangui hissed out an answer.

"Oh! Yes, they were here. They just went that way a few minutes ago."

Nyokabi's mind reeled. Why would mama Wangui lie to the home guards? She stole a glance at Wangui, who gave her a subtle shake of the head. A flicker of understanding dawned on Nyokabi. This wasn't just about protecting food; it was about protecting lives. The weight of their situation pressed down on her. If the home guards knew about the recent Mau Mau visit, they might suspect Mama Wangui of sympathizing with them. The consequences could be dire. Nyokabi swallowed hard, caught between the dangers on both sides.

Sister Madonna cleared her voice. "I think it's time to leave," she said. "The rest of the convoy will be arriving at the meeting spot soon."

They walked out of the store, the weight of the encounter with Mama Wangui heavy in the air. The sky was rapidly getting dark, swallowing the landscape in an inky blackness. Nyokabi could hear Mama Wangui closing the store door behind them, the sound echoing in the sudden silence.

As they approached the parked jeep, a shiver ran down Nyokabi's spine. Leaning against the back of the vehicle was a figure, an unnatural stillness radiating from it. As they got closer, Sister Madonna called out to the man. "Hello, can I help you?"

There was no answer, no movement. The home guards tensed, their hands instinctively reaching for their weapons. The one in charge rushed forward, barking orders at him to stop. He approached the figure, gun raised, but there was no motion. He yelled again, the other home guards formed a protective circle around Sister Madonna and Nyokabi.

Then, the horrifying truth dawned on them all. The figure wasn't a man—it was a corpse, a white man by the looks of it. His lifeless body was propped against the jeep like a grotesque marionette. Terror flooded Nyokabi. The Mau Mau. They had to be close by. This was a message, a chilling reminder of their power and their reach.

She darted her eyes around, searching for any sign of movement in the encroaching darkness. The home guards were shouting, their voices a mix of anger and fear. She longed to run back to the store, to check on Mama Wangui and her sisters, but Sister Madonna's grip on her arm tightened, and she was yanked towards the jeep.

The engine roared to life, and they lurched forward, kicking up dust as they sped away. Nyokabi twisted in her seat, desperately trying to pierce the darkness, hoping for a glimpse of a familiar figure. In the distance, she saw three shadowy figures emerge from the forest, their forms silhouetted against the fading light. Mau Mau. They were watching them leave.

Tears welled up in Nyokabi's eyes. What had she gotten herself into? Fear gnawed at her, a cold dread that settled deep in her stomach. She stole a glance at Sister Madonna, whose face was grim in the faint moonlight. Did the nun know something about the dead man? Was she worried about the encounter with the home guards? Nyokabi opened her mouth to ask, but the words died on her lips. The silence in the jeep was thick with tension, broken only by the rhythmic hum of the engine carrying them further and further away from everything she knew.

Chapter 7

Finally, they got to the convent and Nyokabi ran straight to her room. She always felt emotionally drained each time she left the convent and went out to see the real world and meet her people. This time, her emotions were a mixture of fear, anticipation, apprehension, and worry. She had no friends in school or at the convent. Most of the students in her class had dropped out either from being expelled or for fear of the civil war. Some brave boys came to class though. She felt so alone and knew it wasn't going to get any easier.

Most people in the camps thought she had an easy life living with the white missionaries. She closed the door and dropped to the ground. All her emotions showing in her face now. She reached into her pocket and pulled out the piece of paper her mother had given her. She noticed that her hands were shaking as she tried to straighten it.

"The white settlers are looking for a lady whom they say will go to court to testify that Njaba is not the leader of the Mau Mau. There are some people who may come and ask you where to find her. The settlers are trying to find her and make her change her mind and testify against him. They want a Kenyan leader arrested for terrorism as the leader of the terrorist group Mau Mau. The lady's name is *Patricia Wambui, Your mother's sister.

You don't need to be told what to say. We know you are smart enough to know how to handle the situation."

Her mother couldn't have written this note. She didn't know how to read and write. Someone else must have written it and so someone else knew what was going to happen.

Nyokabi stared at the crucifix above her bed, the image of suffering a stark contrast to the plump pillows beneath her head. Her stomach churned, not with hunger, but with a sour knot of guilt. How could she face another meal when she knew men like her father likely gnawed on watery gruel, their bodies already ravaged by hardship? The insistent clanging of the dinner bell felt like a hammer blow to her conscience.

Downstairs, the clatter of cutlery and forced cheer awaited. The thought of Mrs. Doolan, the convent's regular chef, and her meat stew, usually a source of comfort, now repulsed her. Nyokabi squeezed her eyes shut, the image of scrawny prisoners with hollow cheeks replacing the memory of steaming vegetables. For months, she'd memorized the prisoner rations.

Maize meal	13ozs per person per day
Beans	8ozs per person per day
Potatoes	8ozs per person per day
Green Veggies	8ozs per person per day
Veg oil(vit)	1/2ozs per person per day
Salt	1/2ozs per person per day
Meat	2ozs per person every second day.

It was just enough to keep a soul barely clinging to life.

A surge of anger tightened her chest. She thought of all the colonialists who were thinking about reducing these portions. She remembered that one of the colonialists, Mrs. Cook, had written a venomous letter to the Ministry of African Affairs stating:

"My husband and I just spit when we see the huge rations the Mau Mau prisoners get; they can't eat them all. There is so much and then there are the Kikuyu guards with the pittance grudgingly doled out by the government. No wonder the Mau Mau continue from strength to strength."

Nyokabi's fists clenched beneath the thin sheets. The home guards, funded by the likes of Mrs. Cook, patrolled with gleaming rifles, while the freedom fighters defending their land received scraps. Something had to be done. A rebellious thought flickered in her mind, a tiny ember waiting for a single spark to ignite.

A tentative knock shattered the storm brewing within Nyokabi. Sister Madonna's gentle face peeked through the doorway; her eyes filled with concern. "Can I come in?" she asked softly.

Nyokabi could only manage a weak nod, the knot in her throat threatening to choke back any words that dared to form. Sister Madonna understood. She entered the room, her gaze lingering on the untouched bed and the haunted look in Nyokabi's eyes.

"I've noticed you barely touch any food after your visits home," Sister Madonna said, her voice a soothing balm. "Today must be especially difficult. Even I had to take a moment to process what I witnessed during the trip back to the convent. It's all right to feel overwhelmed, Nyokabi."

Nyokabi squeezed her eyes shut, the image of her tearful brother and the cryptic note flashing behind her eyelids. The urge to confess, to unload the crushing weight of her secret, was almost irresistible. But the potential consequences, the danger it posed to her family and herself, held her tongue hostage.

"I see you're not ready to talk," Sister Madonna continued, her voice laced with understanding. "Perhaps a small snack would be better than a full dinner right now? You should eat something, dear."

Nyokabi nodded again, a flicker of gratitude battling with the turmoil within her. Sister Madonna offered a small, sad smile before leaving the room, the click of the door echoing the heavy silence left behind.

Nyokabi listened as the usual dinner chatter continued downstairs. Sister Madonna returned with some bread and soup. Nyokabi dipped the bread and started eating.

"Nyokabi, what do you think was going on with that boy that was staring at you at the reserve?"

"Do you mean Githinji? Oh, I do not know. He was acting strange though."

"That is the most you have said since we left the reserve," Sister Madonna said with a smile.

Nyokabi smiled back.

Sister Madonna continued. "I guess you are not ready to talk about today and that is okay. I will give you some time to process. I want you to know I am here if you need anything."

Nyokabi nodded.

Nyokabi forced down another mouthful of soup, the comforting warmth a stark contrast to the turmoil within. Sister Madonna's gentle questions about Githinji offered a welcome distraction.

"Githinji," Nyokabi mumbled, the name leaving a strange taste on her tongue. "He was acting oddly, distant, almost...afraid."

An inexplicable pull towards him tugged at her, a yearning for connection that surprised even her. Was it simply a desire for normalcy in these chaotic times, or was there something more about this boy, something hidden beneath his guarded exterior?

The image of Githinji flashed in her mind – the way his eyes darted nervously around the reserve, the tense set of his jaw. Could his strangeness be connected to the war, to the secrets she now carried? The thought sent a shiver down her spine, adding another layer to the tangled web of emotions she grappled with.

Sister Madonna's smile held a hint of knowingness as she excused herself. Alone again, Nyokabi's mind drifted.

In the traditional setting, before things changed, she may have been married to him. She started fantasizing about how life would have been if they were married in the traditional setup.

Since the usual traditions could not be practiced anymore. The elders resorted to telling the stories of how things should have been. Nyokabi had listened in when her siblings were going through the teaching before they got married. She tried to apply the Kikuyu customs and traditions to her fantasy with Githinji.

In the early days, the initiates would enter the arena two by two a boy and a girl to give them a chance to know each other better and more intimately. The elder made sure to emphasize the fact that this was not to lead to sexual intercourse. Numerous dances and festivities were organized even after this period by the young people.

The experiences among the initiates during this time formed strong bonds between them and thus the strong sense of brotherhood and sisterhood amongst them grew. They now became one age-group *riika rimwe*. This was also a chance to form friendships. Sometimes a boy would attract multiple girls and they all nicknamed him *Kiombeni* meaning a heartbreaker. When a girl however attracts the attention of more than one boy, the boys fought it out and whoever won, won her over.

A blush crept up Nyokabi's cheeks as she recalled the elders' teachings about intimacy. The concept of ngweko—the sanctioned exploration of desire between consenting couples—felt both forbidden and strangely alluring. It was a world away from the missionaries' rigid teachings of complete abstinence.

Nyokabi stole a glance at her reflection in the water jug. The yearning for Githinji, a yearning that transcended simple friendship, gnawed at her. Could there be a way to bridge the gap between tradition and her burgeoning feelings—a way to experience a closeness that defied the limitations imposed by the convent?

The weight of her circumstances pressed down on her, but a tiny ember of defiance flickered within. Perhaps there was a way to navigate this uncharted territory, a way to explore this nascent attraction without succumbing to the missionaries' fear-mongering. The path wouldn't be easy, but the desire for connection, for a semblance of normalcy in these chaotic times, fueled her determination. Nyokabi drifted to sleep with Githinji in her mind. She wondered how it would feel to have him actually touch her. This was new to her.

Chapter 8

Nyokabi's eyes snapped open, a jolt of surprise replacing the lingering dream. Sunlight streamed through the gaps in the curtains, painting harsh stripes across the room. School. She was supposed to be at school by eight. Panic clawed at her throat as she scrambled to check the clock. 7:30 am. Oversleeping wasn't something she did. Not anymore.

Hurriedly, she threw back the covers and launched into her morning routine. But a snag awaited. her – her usual, crisp uniform had not been placed on the chair. A knot of unease tightened in her stomach. Mwende, the Kamba lady who tirelessly cleaned and cooked for them, always ensured everything was in order. The absence of the uniform meant only one thing–disruption.

As Nyokabi wrestled with a wrinkled blouse, a glance at the calendar confirmed her growing suspicion. Saturday. No school. Relief washed over her. She hurried down stairs and sat at her usual seat at the dining room table. As she settled in to start breakfast, she noticed Sister Madonna exchange a hushed conversation with Mwende. Sister Madonna's gaze then shifted to Nyokabi.

Nyokabi felt a familiar prickle of fear crawl up her spine. The note. It had to be about the note. Her heart hammered against her ribs, a frantic drumbeat in the sudden silence of the room. Taking a deep breath, she forced herself to maintain her composure and smile at the other nuns sitting at the dining table for breakfast, the weight of the unknown message pressing down on her like a physical burden.

Sister Madonna cleared her throat and wiped her mouth with a napkin. Nyokabi, I believe you have a visitor. Nyokabi stiffened thinking about the note her mother had given her. Had they found her auntie? Was someone talking to the authorities? Did someone other than the author and her mother know about the note? She took her last bite, wiped her mouth with a napkin, and excused herself from the table. Sister Madonna did the same and they both walked out of the room.

Nyokabi's breath hitched in her throat. Visitor? The note. Who could it be? Panic threatened to consume her, but Sister Madonna's gentle hand on her shoulder offered a sliver of hope. Perhaps it wasn't what she feared.

Following Mwende towards the library, her heart hammered a frantic rhythm against her ribs. With a deep breath, she steeled herself, pushing down the fear. Sister Madonna's reassuring presence at her side offered a small comfort.

The library door creaked open, revealing not a stern figure of authority, but a woman in a familiar habit with a warm smile gracing her lips. Relief washed over Nyokabi in a wave, so strong it made her knees weak.

"Hallo Nyokabi," the woman greeted, her voice exuding kindness. "My name is Sister Maria. I apologize for the early intrusion, but I needed to meet you before my departure for Nairobi tomorrow. I've heard wonderful things about you, and

I wanted to formally invite you to attend A-level high school, and possibly even university."

A-Level. The words echoed in Nyokabi's mind; a concept as foreign as the moon. Sister Madonna had mentioned it yesterday but she had not even had time to think about it. She'd never even left Central Province, let alone dreamed of venturing beyond the borders. Yet, here stood this woman, casually proposing a future filled with possibilities that seemed too good to be true.

"Sister Maria," Nyokabi managed, her voice barely a whisper, "and then... university?"

"Indeed," Sister Maria beamed. "There's a potential scholarship program for exceptional students like yourself. If all goes well during your high school years, there might be a chance to further your education in the United States."

The United States? The immensity of it all threatened to overwhelm Nyokabi. Leaving the convent, let alone the country, was a concept she'd never dared to contemplate. Excitement battled with a surge of apprehension. This opportunity, so unexpected and thrilling, felt laden with unknown consequences. A new wave of questions flooded her mind. Could she trust this offer? What would it mean for her secret? Could she leave everything behind, even the weight of her burden?

Sister Maria's smile remained warm, but a hint of knowing flickered in her eyes. "We have much to discuss," she said gently. "Perhaps a trip to Nairobi tomorrow? We can get to know each other better, and I can answer any questions you may have."

Nyokabi's mind raced, a whirlwind of thoughts threatening to consume her. A-level. The United States. The vastness of it all felt dizzying. She needed to pack, to secure a pass, to ensure a lifeline to her aunt if necessary. This opportunity, a beacon of hope in these troubled times, was also a tangled web of uncertainties.

Sister Madonna's voice broke through the fog. "I knew Sister Maria would be coming this weekend," she explained gently. "That's why we arranged your visit home yesterday."

Nyokabi stared at her, speechless. A knot of emotions tightened in her chest – gratitude, guilt, a flicker of resentment.

Sensing her turmoil, Sister Madonna continued. "If it would ease your mind, Nyokabi, I would be happy to accompany you on this trip to Nairobi. Perhaps it would be helpful to have a familiar face beside you."

The offer, unexpected yet comforting, brought tears to Nyokabi's eyes. She met Sister Madonna's gaze, a silent thanks passing between them. This newfound support, a lifeline in this uncharted territory, was a flicker of hope amidst the storm.

"Thank you, Sister Madonna," Nyokabi finally managed, her voice thick with emotion. "I... I would be honored if you came with me."

A wave of relief washed over her as Sister Madonna nodded in understanding. The decision, though daunting, was made. I already secured your pass in anticipation of this. So, all you have to do is go upstairs and get ready. In a daze, Nyokabi left sister Madonna and Sister Maria talking in the library.

She made her way upstairs. With trembling hands, she reached for her clothes, the act of packing mirroring the whirlwind within her. Was she packing for a new chapter, or was this a temporary escape, a bag holding her entire life just in case she needed to turn back?

Sleep that night remained elusive. As Nyokabi stared at the ceiling, a tapestry of emotions played across her face—fear, excitement, a gnawing worry about her secret. This trip to Nairobi, a doorway to an unknown future, marked a turning point. The girl who dreamt of normalcy lost to war now faced a world of possibilities, a world that both terrified and exhilarated her. The journey ahead, filled with unknown twists and turns, was about to begin.

Chapter 9

The morning light cast long shadows as Nyokabi descended the stairs, duffel bag clutched tightly in her hand. Sister Maria stood waiting, a small smile crinkling the corners of her eyes. Nyokabi stole a closer look at this woman who held the key to her potential future. Shorter than Nyokabi herself, Sister Maria possessed an air of quiet strength framed by her blue eyes and wisps of blonde hair peeking from beneath her veil.

"Happy," Nyokabi thought, a flicker of something akin to envy tugging at her heart.

"A couple of days," Sister Maria answered in response to Nyokabi's question about their stay in Nairobi. Her voice was gentle, yet a hint of something unsaid lingered in her tone. Nyokabi found herself strangely drawn to this woman, a stark contrast to the wavering comfort she found in Sister Madonna.

As they piled into the waiting car, a pang of guilt stabbed Nyokabi. Two days away from her family, two days where something terrible could transpire, their safety hanging precariously in the balance because of the secret she carried. The weight of her burden felt heavier than ever, a constant shadow threatening to engulf the excitement bubbling within her.

NYOKABI

The journey unfolded before Nyokabi's wide eyes. The familiar red earth roads of the convent grounds gave way to bustling streets, a cacophony of honking horns and shouted greetings. She pressed her nose against the window, soaking in the sights and sounds—beautiful buildings unlike anything she'd ever seen, women in vibrant clothes balancing baskets on their heads, children chasing each other with joyous abandon. This world, so different from the cloistered life she knew, both terrified and exhilarated her. A thousand questions swirled in her mind, a thirst for knowledge battling with the fear of the unknown.

Sister Maria watched her with a knowing smile, a hint of something deeper flickering in her gaze. This journey, Nyokabi realized, was more than just a trip to Nairobi. It was a journey into the unknown, a journey that could reshape her future in ways she could only begin to imagine.

"Africans came to Nairobi to look for jobs," Sister Maria said. "Some who could not do clerical jobs work as gardeners, cooks, or just farm work like taking care of horses. Your friend Wangui's grandfather is a horse breeder."

"Why are they all bare foot?" Nyokabi asked.

"I do not understand the reasoning behind it but most settlers do not allow the workers to wear shoes as they consider it a way of trying to act superior. The other thing you will notice is that the Europeans do not call them by their names and regardless of how old the man is he is called "boy.""

She paused and continued. "Do you know how the Mau Mau was formed?" Without waiting for an answer, she said. "As expected, the Africans became very disturbed by how things were being run and how oppressed they were. That is why some Kikuyu men went into the forest with a code name Mau Mau. In Kikuyu, when you want to say 'Get Out!' you say 'Uma.' So, when you say this word several times for emphasis it sounds like you are saying Mau Mau. They have organized an army to try and fight the Europeans and force them to leave. The Agikuyu have been singled out because of this. This includes the Meru and Embu as it is difficult to tell them apart as their vernacular is similar and they are neighboring tribes. These tribes have been issued with a passport like the one you are carrying. Showing you have permission from the government to move from one place to another.

"Most Africans who came to Nairobi are living in government housing with walls surrounding them and specific gates where guards are kept. The rest of the Agikuyu are kept in what I would like to call for lack of a better word concentration camps. Also, 'to protect them,' the truth is, they are kept in these camps to make sure that there is no support given to the Mau Mau. It is hoped that this will weaken the movement and eventually, it will 'die out.' In my own way, I am trying to help as many smart people like you to rise above this."

Sister Maria turned around and looked directly at Nyokabi. "You will wear shoes," she said." In fact, you will not go anywhere without shoes."

Nyokabi listened intently as Sister Maria painted a disturbing picture of Nairobi. The bustling city which was once a symbol of progress in Nyokabi's mind, now reeked of oppression. Barefoot Africans toiling away, the derogatory term "boy" used for grown men—a stark contrast to the respect elders commanded in her village before colonization.

And then came that revelation about the Mau Mau, the Kikuyu uprising against the British. A shiver ran down her spine. Was this rebellion connected to the reason they were in Nairobi? Did the secret note hold some key to this conflict?

Sister Maria's words held a quiet defiance, a subtle rebellion against the very system she seemed to represent. Her insistence on Nyokabi wearing shoes, a small act in the grand scheme of things, felt symbolic. Was Sister Maria an ally, or was there a deeper motive hidden beneath her gentle demeanor?

As they entered the heart of Nairobi, Nyokabi scanned the streets with newfound awareness. The grand buildings seemed to cast long shadows, hiding secrets in their corners. She saw groups of Africans huddled together; their faces etched with worry. Were they simply weary workers, or were they part of the Mau Mau resistance? The city, once a source of curiosity for her, now felt charged with unseen tension.

The weight of the secret note grew heavier in Nyokabi's pocket. This trip to Nairobi, meant to be a glimpse into a brighter future, had become an unsettling journey into the heart of a conflict she barely understood. With each passing moment, the lines between right and wrong, friend and foe, blurred. One thing was certain: Her life, once a simple existence within the convent walls, was about to be irrevocably changed.

Chapter 10

They pulled up to a beautiful convent. Nyokabi had never seen such intricate work. As expected, she noticed Africans working in the convent's compound, trimming flowers and some ladies were bringing fresh fruits and vegetables in what she presumed was the kitchen. A nun walked up to them and smiled at both Sister Maria and Sister Madonna. Nyokabi noticed that the nurse quickly looked her up and down then turned back to sister Maria with a big smile.

"I am so happy you made it. I am glad you were able to accompany her sister-"

"Madonna," Sister Madonna finished.

"Well, I will show you to your rooms," she responded.

She did not acknowledge Nyokabi at all. Both Sister Madonna and Sister Maria did not move. The nun hesitated. "I am Sister Magareta," nodding toward Sister Madonna, hoping for introductory responses.

Sister Madonna did not respond. The nun stopped and looked at both nuns with confusion in her eyes.

Sister Maria touched Nyokabi's shoulder. "This is Nyokabi. She will be our guest while we are here."

Sister Magareta's face turned as red as a tomato. She nodded slightly toward Nyokabi.

"This way please," she said, leading them into the convent.

NYOKABI

A jolt of anger sparked within Nyokabi as Sister Magareta completely ignored her, her gaze sweeping over her like she was an inconsequential speck of dust. Was it because she was a guest, an outsider in this grand convent? Or was there something more, a hidden reason for the dismissal that sent a shiver down her spine?

Sister Maria's gentle touch on her shoulder offered a modicum of comfort. Her intervention, her insistence on acknowledging Nyokabi, spoke volumes. Did Sister Maria suspect something about Nyokabi's situation, something that warranted this subtle defiance? The question hung heavy in the air.

As Sister Magareta led them through the opulent halls, her hurried steps betrayed a nervous energy. Her earlier confident smile had vanished, replaced by a flush that stained her cheeks a fiery red. Nyokabi stole a glance at Sister Madonna, but her face remained an unreadable mask.

This new environment, with its intricate beauty and unsettling undercurrents, felt like a labyrinth. With each turn, Nyokabi felt increasingly lost, the mystery of Sister Magareta's behavior adding another layer to the growing web of secrets.

A wave of nausea washed over Nyokabi as she sat alone in her sparsely furnished room. The realization hit her like a physical blow: She was being treated differently, judged solely on the color of her skin. A bitter pang of anger mingled with a deep sadness. This was the harsh reality that people like her faced every day, a world she had only known through the sheltered walls of the convent. Tears welled up in her eyes, blurring her vision. This trip to Nairobi, meant to be a chance for a brighter future, was turning into something darker and more complex than she could have ever imagined.

Dinner was an ordeal. While some nuns greeted her with genuine curiosity, others barely concealed their disdain. Their cold stares felt like icy fingers crawling down her spine. Nyokabi retreated to her room early, the weight of the day pressing down on her. Sleep, however, remained elusive. The unfamiliar sounds of the city echoed through the quiet convent, keeping her on edge.

Chapter 11

A rustle outside her door shattered the silence. Whispers, hushed and urgent, drifted through the thin barrier. Curiosity gnawed at her, urging her to investigate. Silently, she crept out of bed and tiptoed towards the door, her heart hammering in her chest.

Peeking through the crack, she saw Sister Maria huddled with two figures in the dim hallway – an African woman and a man with dreadlocks. A jolt of recognition shot through her. They were talking about her aunt, Patricia. The word "testify" hung in the air, sharp and clear.

Suddenly, the purpose of the secret note, the urgency of getting her out of the village, slammed into Nyokabi with the force of a revelation. Without thinking, she pushed the door open, the sound echoing in the stillness. The figures whirled around, startled. The dreadlocked man pointed at her; his eyes wide with surprise.

Relief flooded Sister Maria's face the moment she saw Nyokabi. "Oh, she's alright," she sighed, her voice laced with tension. Nyokabi stood there, frozen, her mind racing. Who were these people? What was Sister Maria doing? Most importantly, what did the secret note truly mean?

Sister Maria quickly recovered her composure and addressed the man and woman. They exchanged a small envelope, their voices dropping to an urgent murmur. "If she needs anything let me know. You know how to get in touch with me."

Then, the two figures vanished into the night. A moment later, a door creaked open down the hall, revealing a cloaked figure who scurried inside and locked the door behind them.

"Thank you, Sister Maria," the figure whispered.

A million questions swirled in Nyokabi's mind. The carefully constructed world she had known was crumbling around her, replaced by a web of secrets and hidden agendas. Taking a deep breath, she turned to Sister Maria, her voice trembling slightly. "What is going on? Who are those people? What are they saying about Patricia?"

Sister Maria pulled Nyokabi into her room. "I need you to understand something. You cannot tell anyone what you just saw here today."

"What is going on?" Nyokabi interrupted

"I am helping some people protect a very important lady who is going to testify on behalf of Njaba. The people that you saw me talking to are very good friends and allies. They risk their freedom and life to get supplies for the Mau Mau as well."

Nyokabi was crying with relief. Her hands were shaking as she pulled the note out of her pocket. "She is my auntie," Nyokabi whispered.

Sister Maria smiled recognizing her handwriting. "I was not sure you got it. I knew who you were. I just wanted to make sure you trusted me before opening up. I wrote this a few months ago to prepare you just in case someone got to you before I did. Don't worry about it. We have her in a safe place now. Also, Wangui and her family are safe. Nothing happened to them when you left them on Friday."

Tears streamed down Nyokabi's face, a torrent of relief washing away the fear and confusion that had gripped her. Her aunt was alive, protected by a network of brave individuals fighting for a cause she barely understood. Sister Maria's embrace felt like a lifeline, a beacon of hope in this storm of revelations.

"They said... they said my aunt is going to testify," Nyokabi managed between sobs, clutching the secret note in her trembling hand.

Sister Maria's smile, though gentle, held a hint of sadness. "Yes, Nyokabi. Your aunt, Patricia, is a very important woman. Her testimony holds the key to Njaba's future, a man who many believe can lead Kenya to independence."

Njaba. The name echoed in Nyokabi's mind, a whisper on the wind during hushed conversations at the convent. Now, it was a tangible force, a symbol of hope for a nation in turmoil.

"But why?" Nyokabi whispered, her voice barely audible. "Why is my aunt so important?"

Sister Maria pulled out a newspaper clipping, tracing her finger along an article. "Patricia is a witness, Nyokabi. She could prove Njaba's innocence in the eyes of the British. They've accused him of being a leader of the Mau Mau, a 'terrorist' organization. But many, like myself, believe he is a symbol of hope, a man fighting for a just cause. She is being hidden in Nairobi at a place called Bahati. She is safe."

The weight of this knowledge settled on Nyokabi's shoulders like a heavy cloak. Her aunt, a simple woman who loved her garden and her family, held the key to a future she could only imagine. Suddenly, the prospect of a comfortable life at a new school seemed insignificant compared to the struggle unfolding around her.

Sister Maria's eyes, filled with a quiet determination, met Nyokabi's. "You understand now, don't you? The risks, the stakes involved."

Nyokabi stared at the newspaper, her heart pounding a frantic rhythm. This journey to Nairobi, a step towards an unknown future, had taken a sharp turn.

"Now try and get some sleep," said Sister Maria. "I have a lot to show you tomorrow."

Chapter 12

It took several hours for Nyokabi to fall asleep. She couldn't wait to return to the central province where it felt more like home. When Nyokabi woke up, she was momentarily confused as she tried to figure out where she was. She got ready for the day and made her way downstairs. No one was in the dining room; the maids were clearing the table. She looked around trying to see if anyone would acknowledge her. She did not know what to do about breakfast.

One of the nuns stood in a corner reading something looked at Nyokabi and then walked away. Nyokabi did not even have a chance to ask her about breakfast. She looked around and everyone was busy doing something. Exacerbated, Nyokabi walked back to her room.

A burning frustration gnawed at Nyokabi as she retreated to her room. The neglect stung, a stark contrast to the warmth she felt from Sister Maria. Was this how everyone outside the convent treated those who looked like her? Tears welled up in her eyes, blurring her vision. The dream of a brighter future in Nairobi was turning into a nightmare of isolation and prejudice.

A knock on the door startled her. Cautiously, she opened it to find a tray with tea and bread, a small gesture that felt like a lifeline. She saw the same lady from the night before. After handing her the tray, she hurriedly walked away as if she did not want anyone to see her.

The afternoon brought a flicker of hope. Sister Maria's voice, laced with concern, cut through the heavy silence. Sister Madonna accompanied her. Nyokabi poured out her tale, the dismissal at breakfast, the loneliness that had draped itself around her like a shroud. Sister Madonna, to her surprise, had tears glistening in her eyes.

"I can't believe this happened," Sister Madonna murmured, her voice heavy with regret. "We should have checked on you."

Sister Maria's presence seemed to shift the atmosphere. "I expected more from Sister Margareta," she said, her voice firm. We had to run an errand early this morning that took longer than we expected." Nyokabi believed sister Maria was sincerely disappointed.

"Come on, Nyokabi," Sister Madonna said gently. "We'll take you into town and get you a proper meal."

A flicker of doubt crossed Sister Maria's face. "She won't be allowed in most restaurants."

Sister Madonna's jaw tightened. "Then we'll find a place that will serve her," she countered. "This is unacceptable."

The brief exchange revealed a hidden tension between the nuns, a crack in the seemingly serene facade of the convent. As they prepared to head out, Nyokabi couldn't help but steal a glance out the window. The bustling city beckoned, a world she was about to enter, but with each passing moment, the lines between friend and foe, protector and oppressor, seemed to blur.

Chapter 13

The A-level high school was a world away from everything Nyokabi knew. Sister Maria, once a beacon of resistance, now felt more like a distant figure, guiding her through the sterile routines of disciplined studies and providing advice on how to be a woman. Gone were the vibrant stories of her childhood. They were replaced by textbooks and regimented schedules. Sister Maria was determined to have her succeed in academia

Nyokabi couldn't help but compare this to the coming-of-age ceremonies described in hushed tones by her mom, tales of vibrant festivals that stretched for months, a shared experience that marked the transition from childhood to adulthood. A pang of longing shot through her. The impersonal lectures on biology couldn't compete with the richness of these traditions, the sense of belonging that came with being part of a riika, a brotherhood or sisterhood forged through shared rituals and secrets passed down through generations.

Her thoughts drifted to Githinji—fantasies about their future together, a future that seemed increasingly distant. As Nyokabi stared out the window at the rows of identical buildings, a sense of isolation washed over her. She craved connection, a sense of belonging that transcended the classroom walls. Perhaps, she thought, the answer to her yearning wasn't just about Githinji, but about finding a way to reconnect with her heritage, with the traditions described in her mom's stories. These stories, filled with the vibrancy of Kikuyu customs, offered a glimpse into a world where Nyokabi's current feelings wouldn't be considered shameful, but a natural part of growing up.

The weight of unspoken desires pressed down on Nyokabi. There was no denying her attraction to Githinji. But reality, like the cold stone walls of the convent, felt far removed from her fantasies. Sister Maria's lessons on purity and self-control echoed in her mind, a stark contrast to the stories of ngweko, a practice that seemed both liberating and forbidden.

Ngweko, the concept of intimate touching without intercourse, offered a tantalizing glimpse into a different world, a world where her feelings wouldn't be seen as shameful, but acknowledged as a natural part of growing up. But was it a world she dared to explore? The convent's rigid rules loomed large, a constant reminder of the consequences of transgression.

A wave of guilt washed over her as she pictured Githinji's face. Was it fair to indulge in these fantasies, knowing the distance that separated them? Yet, the longing wouldn't be quelled. Night after night, she found herself lost in dreams of stolen moments, of gentle touches that danced on the edge of something more.

Torn between the teachings of the convent and the whispers of her heritage, Nyokabi grappled with her desires. Was there a way to reconcile these two worlds, to find a path that honored her cultural identity without defying the rules that governed her life? The answer seemed as obscure as the future itself.

The conflict between the Mau Mau and the settlers had intensified, prompting the government to declare a state of emergency in 1952. So, it had been a long time since Nyokabi had made a trip back to the reserve. She would get word from Sister Maria's associates regarding the well-being of her family. She had discreetly inquired about Githinji and had heard that Githinji had not been seen in the reserve for some time now. The last family member whom she had seen was her uncle Boniface who worked for the East African Standard Newspaper. He lived in Nairobi and he had stopped by on his way back to Fort Hall in 1951 when he was on leave. He had not been allowed to visit after the state of emergency was declared. She heard that he was escorted to Fort Hall by armed guards "for his own protection from the Mau Mau." He had to hold a pass in his hand the entire time. Nyokabi desperately needed to see her family.

The yearning to see her family, to hold her mother and siblings close, became a relentless tide threatening to drown out the convent's teachings of obedience and passivity. A daring plan, fueled by desperation and a flicker of rebellion, began to take root in Nyokabi's mind. Could she find a way to slip back to the reserve, to determine what was happening, and perhaps even find Githinji?

The stakes were high, the dangers real. But the thought of her family, caught in the maelstrom of a conflict they barely understood, fueled her resolve. Looking at Sister Maria, a silent plea formed in her eyes. Would the nun who had become her confidante, her unlikely ally, support such a reckless endeavor?

Chapter 14

The next time Sister Maria had a secret meeting with the mysterious people who were part of the resistance, Nyokabi snuck out of the convent and waited for them to walk out so she could intercept them. She had to find out if anyone knew what happened to Githinji or word about her family.

When she started to walk up to them, someone grabbed her from the back and placed a knife on her neck. A jolt of fear shot through Nyokabi as a rough hand clamped over her mouth. Panic surged through her veins, but before she could scream, a voice cut through the tense silence.

"Hold on, Koigi!" The voice belonged to the man with dreadlocks, a man she vaguely recognized. Relief washed over her as he lowered his hand, a flicker of recognition dawning in his eyes.

"Nyokabi?" he said, disbelief lacing his voice. "What are you doing out here? It's not safe."

His concern felt genuine, pushing back the tide of fear. "I just... I needed to know," she stammered, "is there any word on Githinji from my reserve?"

The question hung heavy in the air. The man stared at her for a long, probing moment, then nodded curtly. A rustle in the bushes sent shivers down her spine. Slowly, a figure emerged, his face obscured by shadows.

NYOKABI

Nyokabi's breath hitched. There was something about the way he moved, the way he held himself, that sent a jolt of recognition through her. Could it be...?

As the figure stepped into the moonlight, the shock nearly knocked the breath out of her lungs. It was Githinji, but a different Githinji. His familiar features were hardened, etched with a newfound determination. Gone were the carefree eyes she once knew. In their place burned a fierce intensity, a reflection of the struggle he was now a part of.

Embarrassment flooded her cheeks. Here she was, a naive schoolgirl, while he was embroiled in a dangerous fight for his people's freedom. Shame battled with a surge of protectiveness. What had driven him to join the Mau Mau? What dangers did he face every day?

Githinji stepped forward, his gaze filled with a mixture of emotions—surprise, anger, and a tenderness that sent a tremor through Nyokabi. "Nyokabi," he said, his voice a low murmur. "You shouldn't be here. It's too dangerous." His words held a weight that hadn't been there before, a protectiveness that spoke volumes.

Nyokabi felt a surge of defiance. For the first time, she saw the conflict not from the sterile safety of the convent but through the eyes of those directly involved.

Githinji just stood there looking at Nyokabi. The others slowly disappeared into the thicket around them. She was finally alone with Githinji. "I have to find out why you hate me so much," Nyokabi said. Githinji just glared at her and clenched his jaws

"Come on Githinji, I am risking getting in trouble being out here, but I have to find out everything that's going on, especially with you."

There was a glint of amusement in Githinji's eyes. "Oh, you are risking getting in trouble?" he said.

Nyokabi realized how that paled in comparison to what Githinji was risking being out in the forest fighting with the Mau Mau. She looked down and did not answer. His amusement was quickly replaced by frustration.

"I just like you very much and I am not sure why you do not like me," she continued.

"You see!" Githinji almost shouted. "You have lost your way. You are here speaking to me in a very direct way and if I didn't know better, I would think you were one of them with no morals or respect. Why do you put yourself out like that?"

"I would very much like to go through the usual process Githinji but it's hard when you are counting minutes."

"Have you matured?" Githinji asked as if changing the topic.

"You know I didn't get circumcised because of school, so why are you making things so difficult?" Nyokabi asked with a pained look on her face.

"Difficult!? I am making things difficult? We are both in this predicament because of me? How about the fact that I have to practice Ngweko with other ladies now because you are not where you are supposed to be?"

"What is that supposed to mean?" Nyokabi countered. "I am where I am supposed to be. I also have to be direct because I am on stolen time."

"Well, having you with the rest of us would have been nice," Githinji said. "Maybe we would have had something. Possibly even gotten married."

A smile escaped Nyokabi's shell. "I cannot get married now. I have to finish school. I still have a year. I will still be in the proper age to get married."

Githinji's features softened. "I know you don't know this but I have had my eye on you for a while. I even went to the mundu mugo (medicine man) to get a love potion for you as soon as I got circumcised because I didn't think you felt the same way. I want you to be my first wife, Nyokabi."

Nyokabi blushed. "I just didn't know you felt that way about me," she said.

A heavy silence descended upon them, thick and suffocating like the night air itself. Nyokabi's heart hammered against her ribs, a frantic counterpoint to the chirping crickets. Shame burned in her cheeks as she realized the recklessness of her actions. She hadn't understood the danger her "directness" posed.

"Githinji," she started, her voice barely a whisper, laced with remorse. "I didn't think..."

He held up a hand, silencing her. "It's not your fault, Nyokabi," he said, his voice gruff but gentle. "This whole situation is out of our control. The fight for freedom, the traditions that bind us... they all cast a long shadow, and sometimes it's hard to see the path ahead."

The harsh reality of his words struck her like a blow. The fight for independence, once a distant concept, now loomed large, a living, breathing entity that threatened to consume everything, including their love. Here, in the quiet of the night—under the cloak of rebellion and the ever-present threat of violence—their dreams felt like delicate flames flickering in a raging storm.

Githinji shifted closer, his voice softening further. "Ngweko... it's a way for couples to express their affection, to connect on a deeper level. But right now, my only concern is your safety. Being here, with me, was a risk you shouldn't have taken."

A pang of jealousy, sharp and unexpected, twisted in Nyokabi's gut. The thought of him practicing Ngweko with another girl, a forced intimacy born out of her absence, was a bitter pill to swallow. Yet, a sliver of understanding bloomed within her. Tradition held a strong pull in their culture, and the fight for freedom demanded sacrifices, even personal ones.

They stood there, a tangle of emotions swirling between them. A silent plea hung in the air: could their love survive the storm that raged around them? Could they find a way to bridge the gap between their dreams for the future and the harsh realities of war? The answer remained elusive, lost in the shadows of uncertainty, but a flicker of hope, fragile yet persistent, flickered to life within Nyokabi. Perhaps, she thought, there was a way for them to navigate this treacherous landscape together. Githinji was explaining how he lived on the edge but Nyokabi could only stare at him.

A glimmer of hope ignited in Nyokabi's eyes. "If I promise..." Githinji's voice trailed off, his gaze sweeping the darkness. A distant rumble, like thunder on the horizon, sent a tremor through her. Was it just the night, or was it something more?

"If I promise to come back once in a while," he continued, his voice now laced with urgency, "to check on you, will you go back inside?"

The weight of his words settled on her like a heavy cloak. The thrill of seeing him, of being so close after what felt like an eternity, warred with the fear that gnawed at her insides. She knew the dangers of being out here, of being caught between the rebels and the authorities. A vision of Sister Maria's disappointed face flashed before her eyes.

"Yes!" she whispered, the word catching in her throat.

His hand reached out, a fleeting touch on her shoulder. The warmth of his fingers sent a jolt through her body, a spark that ignited a firestorm of emotions. It was a touch that spoke of a thousand unspoken words, a yearning that mirrored her own.

She wanted to move closer, to bridge the gap between them, to feel the full embrace she craved. But an invisible barrier held her back. The weight of their circumstances, the precariousness of their situation, formed a tight knot in her stomach.

Githinji stepped back, his smile bittersweet. "Then go back," he said, his voice barely a murmur. "Be careful."

Nyokabi turned, her legs moving on autopilot. Each step away felt like a betrayal, a tearing away from a connection she desperately craved. Yet, with every step, the safety of the convent walls loomed closer, a stark contrast to the danger that pulsed in the night air. As she slipped back into the shadows, a single tear traced a path down her cheek, a silent testament to the conflict that raged within her—a conflict between love, duty, and the fight for a future that seemed as uncertain as the path ahead.

Nyokabi walked back through the convent doorway, the heavy oak door closing with a soft thud that echoed in the stillness of the night. The encounter with Githinji left her in a whirlwind of emotions. Relief battled with a surge of newfound determination.

Seeing Githinji alive, his anger laced with a tenderness that sent shivers down her spine, was a balm to the worry that had gnawed at her for so long. The confirmation that he was safe, that they could still share a stolen glance or a secret touch, fueled a flicker of hope that had been nearly extinguished by fear.

But relief was quickly overshadowed by a newfound determination. Githinji's presence in the Mau Mau, his fierce protectiveness, ripped away the veil of naivety that had clouded her vision. The fight for independence wasn't a distant abstraction; it was a raw, pulsating struggle with real consequences. Shame burned hot in her cheeks as she realized how sheltered her life at the convent had been.

This shame, however, was quickly replaced by a burning resolve. Githinji's words, his frustration at her "directness" echoed in her ears. He was right. The carefree schoolgirl, yearning for stolen moments, had to be left behind. In her place, a new Nyokabi emerged, a young woman filled with quiet determination. She wouldn't be wielding a machete, but her mind, her education, could become a weapon in this fight.

Nervous energy thrummed through her veins. The sterile walls of the convent, once a haven, now felt stifling. Every creak of the floorboards, every rustle of fabric sent her heart into overdrive. The knowledge that Githinji was out there, fighting for a future they both envisioned, spurred her on. She had to act. But how?

Nyokabi's gaze darted around the room, landing on her desk and the worn copy of a history book. A spark ignited in her eyes. The convent walls, once a barrier, could also be a shield. Perhaps there was information she could glean from these books, messages she could discreetly pass on. The weight of the task settled on her shoulders, but for the first time, she felt like she was finally taking control of her own destiny. A seed of rebellion, a dangerous dance on the edge of discovery, took root in her mind. The path ahead was shrouded in uncertainty, but Nyokabi, fueled by a newfound purpose and love, was finally ready to walk it.

Chapter 15

Nyokabi approached sister Maria and asked if she could be included in the meetings with the mau-mau spies. Sister Maria was hesitant but Nyokabi was very persistent. Sister Maria finally gave in and allowed Nyokabi to pass coded messages to the mau-mau as long as she kept up the good grades because she had a plan for her. This was her final year and Sister Maria wanted her to join a select few to go to the United States for university studies. She had continued to see Githinji secretly and she kept him alive by telling him what was going on and what spots he had to avoid. Since they could only talk for several minutes, their relationship was still the same. Githinji looked different and his hair had grown very long.

Becoming a conduit for coded messages, a lifeline for the Mau Mau, was far more thrilling and terrifying than she ever imagined. Sister Maria's trust, laced with a hint of apprehension, fueled a fierce determination within her. Every message relayed, every coded phrase whispered, felt like a tiny act of defiance against the colonial grip on her homeland.

Yet, the joy of aiding the resistance was overshadowed by a gnawing worry about Githinji. Their stolen moments, precious and fleeting, revealed a stark transformation in him. The familiar warmth in his eyes was tinged with a coldness that spoke of unseen horrors. The first time she saw it, a chilling certainty washed over her—he had taken a life!

The unspoken knowledge hung heavy between them. She felt a desperate need to understand the weight he carried. But something held her back, a fear of shattering the fragile connection they clung to. His growing distance, the coldness that seeped into his gaze at times, fueled a chilling doubt. Was their love just a means to an end? Was she merely a source of information, a link to the enemy camp?

The yearning to be by his side, to see the world through his war-torn eyes, gnawed at her. She fantasized about joining him in the forest, sharing the hardships and triumphs of the resistance. But Githinji's unwavering refusal only deepened the chasm between them. Was his protectiveness genuine, or was it a way to keep her at a safe distance, a pawn he couldn't afford to lose?

Nyokabi walked a tightrope, caught between love and responsibility. Her future, Sister Maria's grand plan of studying abroad, seemed like a distant dream, a path that diverged further with every stolen moment with Githinji. As the conflict within her raged, a single question echoed in the quiet corners of her mind: could love survive in a land divided by war?

Chapter 16

Nyokabi stood in front of the mirror, a bittersweet awareness washing over her. Gone was the carefree schoolgirl; in her place stood a woman sculpted by time and responsibility. She traced the curve of her waist, a reminder of the blossoming beauty that sometimes felt like a burden. Githinji's lingering glances, once a source of innocent flirtation, now sent a shiver down her spine tinged with a touch of unease.

The weight of Sister Maria's expectations hung heavy in the air. The dream of marrying Githinji after school, a vision once vibrant and clear, now faded like a forgotten melody. Reality, harsh and unforgiving, had intervened. Githinji remained in the forest; a warrior consumed by the fight for freedom. A pang of loneliness gripped her heart.

The university, once an afterthought, now took on a new light. It wasn't just about education anymore; it was a lifeline, a way to buy time. Time for what, she wasn't sure. Time for the conflict to end? Time for Githinji to return, a changed man perhaps, but one who still held a flicker of their love?

A spur of rebellion sparked within her. Perhaps the university wouldn't just be a waiting game. Maybe it could be a transformation of its own. She could learn, broaden her horizons, and become the kind of woman who could stand beside Githinji, not just as a lover, but as an equal partner in building a new Kenya.

But the uncertainty bit at her. How long would it take for things to change? Weeks? Months? Years? The future stretched before her, a vast unknown territory filled with both promise and peril. Nyokabi took a deep breath, a new resolve hardening her features. She wouldn't wait passively. She would embrace the opportunity, hone her skills, and chart her own course. Whatever the future held, she would face it with courage, with a heart that still held onto love, and a mind determined to carve her own destiny.

The air crackled with a tension Nyokabi had never experienced before. Stepping out of the convent gates, her heart hammered a frantic rhythm against her ribs. The familiar path to their meeting spot seemed to stretch endlessly, each step an eternity. When Githinji emerged from the thicket, a new kind of awareness bloomed within her.

He led her deeper into the woods, the dense foliage filtering the moonlight into emerald pools. Finally, they reached a hidden clearing, a cool river gurgling its way over smooth stones. Without a word, Githinji stripped off his clothes, his movements purposeful, devoid of self-consciousness. He plunged into the icy water, a gasp escaping his lips that echoed in the stillness.

Nyokabi stood rooted to the spot, her gaze drawn to the unfamiliar sight of his bare body. His laughter, a sound she hadn't heard in ages, brought her back to her senses. Heat flooded her cheeks, a mixture of shyness and a strange exhilaration. She stammered out the information, the coded message tumbling out in a rush.

His laughter turned into a chuckle, a genuine sound that warmed her heart. "Nervous because I'm naked?"

"I am sorry," she whispered. "I don't know how to respond or how this is supposed to feel like."

"No need to apologize, Nyokabi," he said, his voice dripping with amusement. "We wouldn't be strangers if things were different, remember? You'd be used to seeing me like this."

The memory of Ngweko, the whispers exchanged amongst the girls at the school, sent a shiver down her spine. Would she ever experience that kind of intimacy with Githinji?

He emerged from the water, droplets clinging to his skin like glistening jewels. He sat down beside her on a smooth rock, his body still gloriously bare. Shame burned in her cheeks, an unwanted barrier preventing her from meeting his gaze. She had no point of reference, no understanding of this closeness—something she sought, yet feared.

Sensing her discomfort, Githinji closed the distance between them. His breath tickled her cheek, warm and inviting. Then, a touch. A finger brushed against her breast, sending a jolt of electricity through her body. It was a touch both gentle and provocative, arousing a yearning she didn't quite understand.

"This is how it feels," he murmured, his voice a husky whisper.

Nyokabi remained speechless, her mind reeling from the whirlwind of emotions. The touch lingered, a spark igniting a fire within her. But before it could fully blaze, Githinji withdrew his hand, a hint of regret in his eyes. "I have to leave," he said, his voice tinged with urgency. "There's no time..."

NYOKABI

The weight of unspoken words hung heavy in the air. Nyokabi longed to reach out, to bridge the gap between them, both physical and emotional. But the forest, their secret haven, was no longer a sanctuary. The specter of danger loomed large, a stark reminder of the war raging outside their secluded haven. Githinji, the warrior bathed in moonlight, was a stark contrast to the carefree boy she once knew. As he melted back into the green embrace of the forest, Nyokabi was left alone, the echo of his touch lingering on her skin, and a heart filled with a yearning for a love that seemed both closer and further away than ever before.

Chapter 17

Hope, like a fragile flame, flickered brightly in Nyokabi's heart. News of Africans gaining seats in the legislative council whispered of progress, of a future inching closer to freedom. Sharing this spark with Githinji, the thought fueled her eagerness as she ventured out to meet the Mau Mau spies a week later.

But the designated spot was devoid of Githinji's familiar figure. Disappointment clawed at her, a cold dread seeping in. In his place stood a man she vaguely recognized, the one she'd seen conversing with Sister Maria in Nairobi the first time she found out about these meetings. His confirmation that Githinji was "occupied" did little to ease her gnawing worry. "Needs to focus on his work," he echoed, the words devoid of warmth, leaving a bitter taste in her mouth.

The walk back to the convent was shrouded in a heavy silence. Yet, as she neared the gates, a jolt of surprise coursed through her. A dead bird lay at her feet, a stark symbol amidst the manicured grounds. Githinji's secret signal, the one he said he would use to let her know he was around! Hope rekindled, fragile but persistent.

A haunting hoot of an owl shattered the stillness. Her breath caught in her throat. There, was a rustle in the bushes. A figure emerged, fleeting yet unmistakable—Githinji. He vanished as quickly as he appeared, disappearing back into the thicket.

Nyokabi's heart hammered a frantic rhythm against her ribs. The hesitation gave way to a fierce determination. She followed the path he carved, guiding her steps.

When they met again, the clearing was bathed in the soft glow of the moon. His words, laced with a quiet desperation, confirmed her worst fears. "They think you're a distraction," he confessed, a tinge of regret coloring his voice. "Perhaps I've... allowed myself to think of you more than is wise. I want to continue to see you and I will find a way."

Nyokabi closed the distance between them, drawn by an invisible force. He met her halfway, his hand reaching out to cup her cheek. She flinched, a momentary fear wavering across her face.

"Don't be scared, Nyokabi," he murmured, his voice a soothing balm. "I would never hurt you. You are already my wife, in my heart, even if the ceremony hasn't taken place. It may be a while before I can see you again. I want a memory of you."

Understanding dawned on Nyokabi. This wasn't just a stolen moment, it was a desperate attempt to hold onto their connection, a future they both yearned for amidst the uncertainty of war. With a newfound resolve, she leaned into him, ready to create a memory that would bridge the distance, a beacon of love in the coming darkness.

Drawn by an unspoken desire, they returned to the familiar clearing by the river. The air crackled with a tension both exhilarating and unnerving. Githinji reached out, his touch a feather-light caress that sent shivers down Nyokabi's spine. He began to undress her, his movements slow and deliberate, as if committing every inch of her to memory. A spark ignited within her, a yearning that blossomed into a full-fledged fire.

With a tenderness that surprised her, he cradled her close. Their connection, forged in stolen moments and whispered secrets, deepened as they explored each other. The night unfolded in a haze of newfound intimacy, a beautiful awakening for Nyokabi.

When the embers of their passion subsided, he held her close, a content sigh escaping his lips.

"There's never been anyone else," he murmured, his voice thick with emotion. "The war... it stole so much from us. But this feels like a promise, Nyokabi. A promise of a future we can still fight for."

He led her to the riverbank, the cool water offering a welcome chance to cleanse herself. Self-conscious, she attempted to wash away the unfamiliar ache between her legs, a reminder of the intensity of their encounter. He watched her silently, his expression unreadable.

"It gets easier..." he said finally, his voice soft. "With time."

Together, they walked back to the edge of the forest. A newfound intimacy bloomed between them, a silent acknowledgment of the bond that had deepened this night. As he disappeared back into the trees, a single tear traced a path down Nyokabi's cheek. It was a tear of pain, a tear of fear for his safety, but also a tear of joy, a bittersweet confirmation of her womanhood and the love that bloomed amidst the chaos. The memory of this night, forever etched into her heart, would be a beacon, a reminder of the love they shared, a love they fought for in a world teetering on the edge.

Their stolen moments became a cherished routine for Nyokabi. Githinji materialized from the forest several times that month, a beacon of warmth in the encroaching cold. Knowing their time together was dwindling before her month-long visit home, Nyokabi devised a plan for a final night under the stars.

That night stretched into a tapestry of whispered secrets and passionate embraces. They made love under the vast, indifferent sky, the twinkling stars their only witnesses. Returning to the convent before dawn, she felt a pang of bittersweet relief. The cold, while biting, seemed insignificant compared to the fire that burned within her. How did Githinji endure the elements, the harshness of the forest, especially as the chill deepened? A fierce admiration bloomed alongside her love.

Their love, nurtured in stolen moments, had blossomed into something profound, an anchor in their turbulent world. The looming separation cast a shadow, but they clung to possibilities. Law school, Sister Maria had proposed, a path for Nyokabi to contribute to a future Kenya, a nation governed by its own people.

Chapter 18

The remaining months stretched before her; each day was precious. Sister Maria began the meticulous process of securing Nyokabi's future abroad. A bittersweet cocktail of excitement and trepidation swirled within her. New horizons beckoned, yet the thought of leaving Githinji behind tore at her heart. Would their love bridge the miles? Would they find their way back to each other amidst the winds of change sweeping their nation? These were unanswered questions, a testament to the enduring power of love in the face of uncertainty.

The weight of impending departure hung heavy as Nyokabi prepared to return home. This school break marked the final chapter before her final term. Having aced her university entrance exam, all that stood between her and America was one final hurdle—her final exams. Sister Maria, a pillar of unwavering support, had already set the wheels in motion for her studies abroad.

Packing was a bittersweet affair. Each familiar item held a memory, a reminder of the life she was leaving behind. As Sister Madonna arrived to ferry her back to the reserve, a glimmer of hope sparked within Nyokabi. Perhaps a familiar face, someone from Githinji's family, would be a balm for her yearning. Of course, her love remained a closely guarded secret, but even a glimpse of his kin would offer a sense of connection.

The journey to the reserve passed uneventfully, the familiar landscape blurring by. Arriving at the camp, a wave of nostalgia washed over her. Her eyes scanned the surroundings, searching for a comforting presence, a connection to Githinji. Disappointment tugged at her heart, but she found solace in the warmth of her family's embrace. Nyokabi and Sister Madonna were greeted with the same enthusiasm as always. Mama Nyokabi retreated to her hut and welcomed Sister Madonna in. Nyokabi excused herself and followed her dad.

Following tradition, her father lived in a separate hut from his wives. Nyokabi sought a private audience with her father in his hut. As they walked to the hut, she exchanged greetings with one of her step-mothers, she waited patiently for everyone to walk away. Now alone with her father, a sense of urgency bubbled within her.

"Dad," she began, her voice filled with a mix of excitement and apprehension, "my time at the advanced-level high school has been an incredible learning experience."

Her father's smile was warm, tinged with a hint of sadness. "I missed you, Nyokabi. These past years have been fraught with danger, especially since the state of emergency was declared. I trust you received my messages?"

She nodded, the weight of his unspoken message settling on her shoulders. "It's been hard not seeing you as often as I'd like," he acknowledged, his voice low. Nyokabi's father had expressed his admiration and pride in Nyokabi's secret meetings with the Mau Mau.

"I've been doing my part, however small, in the fight for freedom. Passing coded messages for the Mau Mau is my way of striking a blow against the colonial regime." Nyokabi said. I believe in my absence Sister Maria will continue with the work."

"Leaving the country will be a wrenching separation, but ultimately a necessary sacrifice. Kenya needs strong, intelligent women like you, Nyokabi. You are our hope for a brighter tomorrow. Your mother has also been playing her part in the struggle."

Nyokabi felt a surge of respect for her parents, their dedication to the cause mirroring her own growing sense of purpose. Her father's words served as a gentle nudge, a confirmation of the path she was about to embark on.

"I understand, Dad," she replied, her voice gaining strength. "I know I need a purpose, a reason for leaving. An education will be my weapon, my way to contribute when I return."

A sudden shift in her emotions prompted her to change the subject. "Dad," she asked, her voice catching, "why did Baba Njuguna take his own life? There are rumors, but I need to know the truth. What's happening to our people?"

Her father looked at her, his gaze filled with a mixture of pain and pride. The weight of the answer hung in the air, a silent promise of a difficult conversation to come. This was just the beginning, Nyokabi knew. There would be stories to share, burdens to bear, and a future to fight for, a future she would face head-on, armed with love, knowledge, and the unwavering spirit of her people.

A heavy silence descended upon the hut. Nyokabi's father steepled his fingers, his brow furrowed in a deep internal struggle. It was clear the weight of the story he was about to tell pressed heavily on him. Finally, with a resigned sigh, he spoke.

"Njuguna joined the Mau Mau," he began, his voice low and heavy. "He believed in their fight for freedom, and for a while, there was hope. But the colonialists responded harshly. They enacted a law—the Terrorist Land Forfeiture Act—that stripped land away from anyone suspected of Mau Mau affiliation."

Nyokabi felt a knot of dread tighten in her stomach. Land, in her culture, was more than just property; it was identity and legacy. To lose it was a devastating blow.

Her father continued; his voice laced with sorrow. "They took everything, Nyokabi. His land, his livelihood—all claimed as unpaid taxes. Baba Njuguna felt a crushing sense of shame. He believed he had failed his family, that he had nothing left to offer his wives."

A flash of something other than sadness crossed her father's eyes – a glint of anger, perhaps, or a burning sense of injustice. Nyokabi understood. The humiliation, the helplessness; it must have been a suffocating weight for a proud man to bear.

"They were coming for him the next day," her father said, his voice barely a whisper. "Accused of tax evasion, a convenient excuse. He... he chose his own fate. Death, it seemed, was preferable to the public humiliation that awaited him."

Nyokabi's world shrunk. The respected elder, Baba Njuguna, was reduced to such a desperate end. Anger simmered within her; a potent cocktail mixed with grief. The fight for freedom, it seemed, came at a terrible cost. But amidst the pain, a seed of resolve hardened within her. Baba Njuguna's story, a stark reminder of the brutality they faced, fueled a silent vow. She would not let his sacrifice be in vain. She would get her education, and she would return, armed with knowledge and a burning desire to build a future where such injustices would never happen again.

The realization struck Nyokabi with the force of a physical blow. "No wonder Githinji joined his brother, Njuguna in the fight," she whispered, the unspoken words hanging heavy in the air. The weight of Baba Njuguna's story, his tragic end, resonated deeply within her. It was a missing piece of the puzzle, a stark explanation for Githinji's fierce determination, and his unwavering commitment to the Mau Mau.

Her father, watching her closely, saw the dawning comprehension in her eyes. He knew then that the weight of their struggle, the human cost of their fight for freedom, could no longer be shielded from her. A silent understanding passed between them; a shared burden that bound them closer.

At that moment, Nyokabi's resolve solidified into a burning ember. Her education, once a path to a secure future, now transformed into a weapon. The knowledge she would gain wouldn't just be for her own advancement; it would be a tool to dismantle the oppressive system that had driven a good man like Baba Njuguna, a once proud elder reduced to a desperate suicide.

The image of Githinji, his eyes blazing with a similar fire, surfaced in her mind. He was out there, fighting not just for a nation's freedom, but for the dignity of his people, for a future where such tragedies wouldn't become commonplace. A surge of fierce love and admiration washed over her. The path ahead would be difficult, fraught with uncertainty, but she would walk it, her heart filled with the memory of Baba Njuguna's sacrifice and the unwavering love for the man who fought in his memory.

Chapter 19

A knot of worry tightened in Nyokabi's stomach as she realized she hadn't seen her little brother, Mburu. Finding her mother, her face etched with concern, Nyokabi learned that Mburu wasn't feeling well. Sister Madonna, ever the pragmatist, suggested taking him to the mission hospital and offered to leverage her connections to arrange his transport back with the guards.

Seized by a wave of tenderness, Nyokabi volunteered to dress Mburu. It was a small act, a silent apology for the inattention caused by her own divided loyalties. Cradling her brother in her arms, she felt a surge of protectiveness, a fierce love that transcended the turmoil swirling around her.

At the hospital, the sight of a nurse rushing to attend to them, a privilege undoubtedly secured by Sister Madonna's presence, sent a jolt through Nyokabi. A tide of conflicting emotions rose within her. Relief battled with a prick of shame as she noticed the accusatory stares of other patients waiting patiently for care. The weight of her growing estrangement from her people pressed down on her, a heavy counterpoint to her desperate desire to protect those she loved – her parents, her brother, the members of the Mau Mau, and of course, Githinji. She clung to the belief that by helping those within her reach, she was contributing in some way to a larger cause.

Mburu's diagnosis of malaria brought a fresh wave of terror. As she held him close, his feverish body a stark contrast to her own cool skin, a primal maternal instinct roared within her. She would bear any burden, face any danger, to shield him from harm. Sister Madonna's comforting words, a gentle reminder of faith and hope, offered a sliver of solace.

Nyokabi made a silent vow. She would do everything in her power to ensure Mburu's well-being, to pave the way for a future filled with the "great things" that sister Madonna had spoken of. The experience at the hospital, with its glaring contrast between privilege and hardship, served as a burning indictment of the inequalities that plagued her world. It was a weight she would carry with her, a burden that would fuel her resolve to build a better future, not just for her family and loved ones, but for all who yearned for a more just and equitable society.

The drive back to the reserve was shrouded in Nyokabi's concern for Mburu. The offer from the police escort to relieve her of carrying him was met with a resolute refusal. The weight of her earlier inattention, a time when he was most vulnerable, pressed heavily on her. Cradling him close now, the warmth of his feverish body a stark contrast to her own, offered a precious chance for solace, a stolen moment of connection before the ordeal at the hospital.

Sister Madonna, with her keen awareness of time, interjected with a reminder of their planned stay at the convent that night because she was going to help Nyokabi with her assignment the next day. "We have an early start tomorrow," she cautioned, "and dinner will be out of the question. Perhaps we can grab a bite on the way back?"

The suggestion resonated with Nyokabi, but only because it meant delaying the inevitable separation from Mburu, even for a short while. The prospect of a familiar face, a brief respite from the turmoil that surrounded them, held a sliver of comfort. She longed for a connection to normalcy, and Mama Wangui's shop represented that fragile thread. Sister Madonna, ever accommodating, readily agreed.

As dusk settled over the camp, they were met with the sight of police conducting a meticulous screening of every male over the age of fourteen. A stark reminder of the ever-present tension. The suspected presence of Mau Mau cast a long shadow. Nyokabi and Sister Madonna were forced to wait patiently as the security checks were meticulously completed.

By the time they reached Mama Nyokabi and explained the medication regimen for Mburu, the last rays of daylight had surrendered to the inky embrace of night. The additional stop at Mama Wangui's and the return trip to the convent loomed before them, yet another hurdle in a day already overflowing with worry and delay. But Nyokabi pressed on, fueled by her unwavering love for her brother and the weight of her responsibilities, a burden she carried with quiet determination.

Chapter 20

The return trip to the convent was shrouded in a suffocating silence, punctuated only by the rhythmic hum of the jeep's engine. Darkness had draped itself over the land, deepening the sense of foreboding that gnawed at Nyokabi and Sister Madonna. Each woman, a prisoner of her own churning thoughts, grappled with the tense reality that enfolded them. Nyokabi glanced at Sister Madonna, a silent question flickering in her eyes. The subtle movement of the nun's lips, a murmured prayer for safe passage, offered a fragile comfort in the face of the unknown.

Their arrival at Mama Wangui's shop was met with a scene that sent a jolt of trepidation through Nyokabi. The sight of Wangui and her sister huddled beneath empty sugar sacks sent a tremor of unease down her spine. It was an unspoken sign, a chilling suggestion of the Mau Mau's proximity. The forced cheerfulness that colored their greetings, the hurriedness in Mama Wangui's demeanor – it all painted a picture of disquiet. Nyokabi's senses were on high alert, a primal instinct screaming danger. The once friendly shopkeeper seemed distant, her gaze flickering away from theirs, a subtle shift that spoke volumes.

As they hurriedly consumed their meals, of Ngwashe (sweet potatoes) and milk, a raw tension crackled in the air, thick enough to choke on. Nyokabi couldn't shake the feeling of being watched, a prickling sensation that danced across her skin. A flicker of movement in the periphery of her vision, a fleeting shadow amongst the bushes, sent shivers down her spine. She froze, her gaze darting nervously around the darkening landscape. The guards, mirroring her unease, had their weapons drawn, a silent acknowledgment of the lurking threat.

The sight of Sister Madonna's ashen face, a stark contrast to her usual composed demeanor, confirmed Nyokabi's worst fears. Even the stoic nun wasn't immune to the terror that stalked them in the night. News of the horrors inflicted on settlers filtered through the grapevine, reaching even the most remote corners of the country, a chilling reminder of the brutality that could erupt at any moment.

The Mau Mau's fight for independence, a noble cause in its essence, was stained by the violence that shadowed their actions. The Lari massacre, a gruesome tableau of Kikuyu deaths, served as a stark warning. Though the Mau Mau denied responsibility, the weight of that tragedy hung heavy in the air, a constant reminder of the unforgiving consequences of betrayal. In this climate of fear and suspicion, everyone walked a tightrope, their actions under constant scrutiny, their loyalties a matter of life and death.

The metallic clang of the jeep door slammed shut echoed in the tense silence. As Nyokabi reached for the handle, a barely audible creak from Mama Wangui closing her shop sent a jolt of terror through her. It was a confirmation of her worst fears, a chilling premonition of what was about to unfold.

Before she could even scream a warning, figures materialized from the shadows like phantoms. Wild-eyed men, their faces etched with a savage intensity, materialized around them. The ragged clothes and untamed hair, an indications of a life lived on the fringes and dedication to their cause.

Fear, cold and sharp, clawed at Nyokabi's throat. One of the men, his eyes blazing with a frightening zeal, grabbed Sister Madonna, holding her hostage. The others kept their guns trained on the guards; their fingers twitchy on the triggers. A barrage of questions, laced with suspicion and barely veiled menace, ripped through the night air.

Nyokabi opened her mouth to plead, to offer some explanation, some reason for their presence. But her voice, usually strong and clear, had deserted her. The men were a terrifying spectacle, each twitch of a muscle, each glint of metal, a terrifying reminder of their precarious situation.

Chaos erupted. A sickening thud echoed through the night as one of the guards was struck with the butt of a gun. A deafening gunshot, shot in the air followed, shattering the fragile peace. In the blink of an eye, the world dissolved into a blur of terror. A warmth spread through Nyokabi's legs, a coppery tang filling her nostrils. She couldn't bring herself to look, the fear paralyzing her. This was it. This was how it ended.

Then, a new figure emerged from the darkness. He walked with a swagger, a strange smile playing on his lips, a stark contrast to the grim expressions of his comrades. Hesitantly, Nyokabi met his gaze. Though his face was obscured by the shadows, a flicker of recognition sparked deep within her. Those eyes, they held a familiar warmth, a faint echo of someone she cherished. It was Njuguna, Githinji's brother.

He approached the leader, a hushed conversation passing between them. Nyokabi couldn't make out the words, but a shift occurred, a subtle change in the atmosphere. Njuguna cast a final, enigmatic smile in her direction before disappearing back into the undergrowth. As if on cue, the rest of the Mau Mau melted away into the darkness, their movements swift and silent, as if they were phantoms returning to the night.

The silence that descended was thick and heavy, broken only by the moans of the wounded guard and the metallic tang of blood in the air. Nyokabi stared, dumbfounded, at the scene that unfolded before her. They were alive. Somehow, against all odds, they had survived.

A strange mix of emotions washed over her. Relief, tinged with a sliver of shame for the involuntary reaction that had stained her clothes. Gratitude for Njuguna's intervention, a silent act that spoke volumes about his loyalties and his unspoken concern for her. And most importantly, a spark of excitement, a thrill that danced beneath the surface of her fear. She had seen him, a fleeting glimpse of Githinji's brother, a connection to the man who held her heart captive.

The journey back to the convent was shrouded in a somber silence. The ordeal had left them shaken, the weight of the encounter clinging to them like a shroud. Ahead lay a long night, a night for reflection and trepidation.

Yet, amidst the fear, a tiny seed of hope bloomed within Nyokabi. Though a month stretched before her, a month of separation from Githinji, the encounter with Njuguna was a bridge, a fragile connection that offered a flicker of comfort in the face of uncertainty. She had faced her fear, and in doing so, she had unknowingly played a part in their survival. This experience, harrowing as it was, had irrevocably altered the course of her journey, weaving her fate even more tightly with the fight for freedom and the man she loved.

Chapter 21

Nyokabi woke up one morning and walked out her mother's hut. She had been here a few days. She noticed people talking in hushed tones. Mau Mau was mentioned and her dad was shaking his head as if in disbelief. Mama Njuguna had tears running down her face. Nyokabi felt a chill going down her spine. Had something happened to Njuguna or worse...Githinji? She walked up to the ladies around Mama Njuguna.

"They killed several of them. Someone must have betrayed them," one lady was saying.

Nyokabi froze. Her mom leaned closer to Mama Njuguna. "It doesn't mean your boys are among those who were killed," she said. Mama Njuguna did not find any consolation in those words.

"I need to see my boys and make sure they are okay," Mama Njuguna responded.

Nyokabi let out a slow breath. She needed to find out if Githinji and his brother were safe. She could not talk to anyone about Githinji or their relationship. She had to keep it is secret. She knew he was always in constant danger but she hoped that they would survive this war and that they would both be living a fulfilling life after Kenya gained her independence. Nyokabi could not wait to go back to school. She had to go back to

Githinji and their secret meetings. For now, she had to find a way to calm her fears.

Nyokabi's heart pounded in her chest. The news of the killings hung heavy in the air, a suffocating weight that squeezed the hope out of her. She stole a glance at Mama Njuguna, her face etched with worry, and knew she had to be strong.

Taking a deep breath, Nyokabi walked up to Mama Njuguna knelt beside her. "Mama Njuguna," she said softly, her voice barely a whisper. "Let me go see if I can find Baba. Maybe the villagers can tell us what happened."

Mama Njuguna's eyes widened, a flicker of fear crossing her face. "No, Nyokabi. It's too dangerous. They might be..." Her voice trailed off, unable to voice the terrifying possibility.

Nyokabi squeezed Mama Njuguna's hand reassuringly. "I'll be careful, Mama Njuguna. I know it's risky, but we can't just sit here and wait in fear. If they are safe, it will ease your heart, and if not, we'll face it together. You're not alone in this."

Mama Njuguna hesitated; the internal struggle evident on her face. The yearning for news of her sons warring with the fear for Nyokabi's safety. Finally, she nodded slowly, a tear rolling down her cheek. "Be very careful, Nyokabi. And come back quickly, no matter what you find."

Emboldened by Mama Njuguna's hesitant permission, Nyokabi rose to her feet. Her mind raced with possibilities. Where would she find news and will her dad be suspicious about her asking questions regarding Njuguna and Githinji? Would they be together, or scattered by the violence? Steeling herself, she formulated a plan.

"I'll start by asking around the village," she told Mama Njuguna. "Someone might have seen them or know where they might be."

With a final nod and a silent prayer, Mama Njuguna watched Nyokabi disappear into the throng of villagers, their hushed voices swirling around them like a swarm of worried bees.

Dread coiled around Nyokabi's heart like a venomous snake. The reserve, usually abuzz with life, seemed shrouded in an unsettling silence. Her attempts to gather information yielded nothing but worried whispers and blank stares. The overheard conversation about a Mau Mau ambush, the chilling figure of thirty dead, sent a wave of nausea crashing over her.

Githinji. The name echoed in her mind; a frantic prayer whispered on a trembling breath. The possibility of him being among those hunted down, silenced forever, was a terrifying thought. She knew the harsh realities of the conflict – the secrecy, the sacrifices, the ever-present danger. Even if he and Njuguna were alive, communication would be a treacherous dance. A stolen glance, a cryptic message passed through a trusted third party – these were the only channels open to them at this time, fraught with the risk of exposure and brutal consequences.

The weight of the unknown pressed down on her. Returning to school felt like an eternity. It was her only hope, a fragile thread connecting her to Githinji. She would try and go to their spot and hopefully connect with him and just the thought of that gave her a flicker of reassurance.

Chapter 22

The days stretched before her, each one an agonizing test of her patience. The image of Githinji, his eyes blazing with determination, fueled a silent resolve within her. She would wait, endure the uncertainty, and find a way to connect. This fight for freedom, for their future together, demanded courage, sacrifice, and an unwavering spirit. And Nyokabi, fueled by love and a growing sense of purpose, was determined to possess them all.

Finally, the day came for Nyokabi to return to school. Those preceding days had been really hard on her. She still had no news regarding Githinji's fate. She had only read a newspaper clipping brought to her by one of the villagers. They hoped that she could read it and that it would have answers to their questions. But all it said was;

The Mau Mau resistance frightened the Europeans and in 1950 it was banned by the government. In 1952, the government declared a Mau Mau state of emergency. The Mau Mau's main aim was to force the white settlers to go, it was obviously not their aim to kill them because only a small number of settlers were killed and it would have been easy to kill more.

Sir Evelyn Baring, the new governor who arrived in 1952, examined the facts of more than twenty-three probable Mau Mau murders, including that of a chief who was killed during the day, seven miles from Nairobi.

He asked for British Troops and arrested Njaaba and 98 others. Njaaba was obviously not the Mau Mau leader, but the government insisted that there were links between K.U.A.S and Mau Mau, and that was enough to involve him. He was tried, found guilty, and sentenced to seven years in Prison. The validity of this trial is obviously questionable.

Patricia was arrested for testifying that Njaaba was not the leader of Mau Mau. She was picked up in a helicopter and was tortured. She was threatened that she would be dropped from the helicopter if she did not change her mind and testify against Njaaba but she is a strong woman.

The Mau Mau movement is opposed to the treatment of Africans merely as labor machines and less than men. It is particularly opposed to the possession of lands on 999-year leases, some of which belong to the Agikuyu.

Now to 'protect' the Agikuyu they were transported to places, more like concentration camps. All boys fourteen years and above are screened for any association with the Mau Mau. At this point, the Kikuyu, Embu, and Meru were given a passport, and their every movement was monitored. They have to get a pass-more or less like a visa to visit a place different from their camp. Those who work in Nairobi have to get a visa to visit their families in the camps and vise versa.

There are some camps that are specifically for holding suspects temporarily for 24 hrs or 48 hrs on weekends. They are all over the country. In the central province alone there are 156 camps.

There are several interrogation centers including Dr. Becker's Lamu house. It was proposed that there should at least be one interrogation center per location. They are all going to be under European supervision.

Finally, the fate of her auntie after testifying was known to Nyokabi. Everything else was old news.

She finally made it back to school. Her first day of school was busy. She had to supervise clean up. The girls had to clean their bathrooms and class rooms. Even though Nyokabi lived with the nuns and not in the dorms like the other younger girls, she had to be involved in the clean-up. She also had to make sure the boys cleared the bush near their dorms and class rooms and later on everyone carried the dirt to a pit and burned it.

By the time all was done, it was dinner time. Most of the girls went and took showers before dinner. Everything was going well until one girl started screaming. Nyokabi froze when she heard the scream. She finally recovered and started running in the direction of the scream. The girl looked shaken, but fine. She was sitting on her bed crying. There was a crowd now around the girl.

"What is it?" Nyokabi asked.

"There was a scary-looking man at the window. He must be a member of the Mau Mau. He looked dead at me and then disappeared. He was carrying a dead bird, he dropped it when I started to scream and disappeared into the night."

Nyokabi felt faint. She had to think fast.

"Who else saw him?" Nyokabi asked.

"No one. I was the last in here. everyone had left for the dining room. I was just getting ready to leave when I heard a noise. I stopped and walked to the window to see what it was. He must have thought no one was here because he looked surprised. Maybe he wanted to hide in here and rape us while we slept. I am sure he wasn't alone."

The guards and some nuns had already walked into the room. They heard the entire story.

One nun took the girl by the hand and said, "Let's go and talk to Sister Maria." She turned toward the guards and said, "You stay here until we get to the bottom of this."

Nyokabi didn't know what to do. She knew that must have been Githinji. Although relieved that he was alive, she was afraid for him but also felt like she had to see him. Still the thought of Githinji being so close excited her. She had to find a way of going to him. She had to see him!

Chapter 23

There was a lot of excitement that evening. The guards were increased at the school. Nyokabi had to find Githinji before bedtime. She was not sure it would be safe to sneak out at all. She had to disappear when everyone was busy.

Her chance came when Sister Maria announced there would be an assembly before bedtime. No one would notice she was not there and everyone's attention would be on what was going on. No one would attempt to walk alone in the dark after what had just happened.

She waited for the bell to ring. Everyone started moving towards the hall. She sneaked and hid behind a bush and when all was clear, she ran to the spot where they met. Githinji's hair was wet. He must have already bathed. He was hiding behind a bush. She smiled and started undressing.

"I am so happy to see you!" she said. "I was worried about you and Njuguna. I heard about the ambush."

"I am fine. Unfortunately, Njuguna did not make it...." His voice started to trail.

Nyokabi reached out to him and embraced him. "I am so sorry," Nyokabi said.

He nodded and as if melting into her he moved even closer to her. Nyokabi continued to undress. Githinji smiled knowingly through his sadness and started undressing too.

Back at the assembly, Sister Maria went through the safety drill. The guards were told not to allow anyone out of the dorm until morning. The police would comb the forest around the school thoroughly. Mbugua was the head boy and he was called to the front and was given instructions on how to keep the boys safe. Nyokabi was called to the front. Of course, she was not in the hall.

"Nyokabi! Where is Nyokabi?" Sister Maria asked, prompting everyone to look around.

"Has anyone seen Nyokabi?" she asked. When no one answered, she said, "Something must have happened to her. Everyone stay here! Guards, let's go find her!"

They walked out into the night with lanterns. The guards had their guns ready. They were expecting anything. They went to the sleeping quarters at the convent first. They called out her name but there was no response. Sister Maria was white as a sheet. She started to pray. Some of the nuns had their rosaries in hand and they were fondling their beads.

Some guards walked into the bushes and cautiously started combing through them with their guns at the ready. Soon they were in the forest walking noiselessly and looking.

Chapter 24

Nyokabi and Githinji were both naked now. He said, "I thought the girl I scared would spoil everything. I didn't think you were coming. You took so long."

Nyokabi smiled and said, "I had to wait until it was safe to get away. Everyone thinks the Mau Mau are here and ready to attack. Everyone is scared. They are having an assembly now. No one will miss me, but I have to sneak back into the assembly before anyone does."

Githinji smiled lowered her to the ground and he became one with her.

There was a noise in the bush. Githinji stopped; he looked around but Nyokabi pulled him back towards her. "It's probably just a rabbit or something," she whispered.

He turned his attention back to her. He continued making love to her.

"Hey!" someone yelled. Soon there was a light shining on them. They froze and looked up at the guards.

Sister Maria's heart pounded in her chest, mirroring the frantic pace of her steps as she strained to catch up to the guards. The scene that unfolded before her was a horrifying tableau – a sickening mix of recognition, fear, and a crushing disappointment that contorted her features. "Wait!" she screamed, her voice a desperate plea lost in the cacophony of the night.

Githinji stood paralyzed, his hands raised in a futile gesture of surrender, a flicker of shame warring with defiance in his eyes. Beside him, Nyokabi trembled, her vulnerability laid bare. Instinctively, she tried to shield her nakedness and ran towards the bushes to hide. A branch cut her forearm and blood started to ooze down her arm but she did not notice it.

Githinji snatched a stick and hurled it with all his might at the closest guard. The blow landed true, a sickening thud echoing through the night as the guard crumpled to the ground.

But it was a fatal miscalculation. Before Githinji could even contemplate raising the fallen guard's gun, a hail of bullets erupted from the darkness. His body buckled slowly, crumpling to the ground like a discarded rag doll. His eyes, filled with a heartbreaking mixture of love and apology, remained fixed on Nyokabi in a silent farewell. The guards, adrenaline coursing through them, continued firing even after he lay motionless, a gruesome display of excessive force that painted the night a grotesque shade of red.

Nyokabi's world shattered. A primal scream, laced with raw grief and disbelief, erupted from her throat. Sister Maria, her face etched with a motherly concern and pain, engulfed the young woman in a desperate embrace.

The hysterical cries, the lifeless body of the boy she loved sprawled at her feet—it was too much to bear.

As the gunfire died down, all eyes turned to the distraught Nyokabi. She seemed to have lost her mind. She was screaming and fighting to get to Githinji's motionless body. Sister Maria was holding her but her efforts were dwindling. One of the nuns had finally succeeded in covering her naked body. She had tied Nyokabi's skirt around her waist. She joined Sister Maria in trying to stop Nyokabi from running towards Githinji's body.

They tried to turn her away and walk back to the school but she pushed them away. She didn't care that she was half-naked. Eventually, another nun joined in and they half dragged her, half carried her back to the school.

They took her to Sister Maria's office. Only the nuns were in the office. Nyokabi was still crying. She was covered up now.

"How could that man come so close to the girls?" one of the nuns said. "He must have had the intention of raping the girls because he didn't run away even after he knew he had been spotted."

"It is a pity it had to be Nyokabi," another one said.

"Yeah, she may never recover from this," the third one chimed in.

"Maybe she screamed, but no one heard," the first one continued. "By the time we got to her, she must have resigned herself to her fate."

"Poor girl, she can't even speak," someone said.

"Ladies, could you please excuse us for a moment," Sister Maria said.

Sister Maria, her resolve hardening like steel, dismissed the other nuns with a curt nod. The office became a sanctuary of silent grief. Nyokabi remained oblivious to the whispers of pity and speculation swirling around her like vultures. The weight of tragedy had stolen her voice, leaving behind a hollow shell of a girl.

Sister Maria, the sole witness to Nyokabi's silent torment, knew the road to healing would be long and arduous. The trauma, etched deep within Nyokabi's soul, would demand compassion, understanding, and a safe space to grieve.

In the sterile confines of the office, amidst the judgmental whispers, Sister Maria vowed to be that sanctuary, a beacon of hope in Nyokabi's darkest hour.

"I wish I knew what was going on, I would have protected you both," she whispered almost to herself.

Chapter 25

The next few months crawled by. Nyokabi remained in a haze of grief. Her once bright eyes dimmed, reflecting a hollowness that mirrored the cavern left by Githinji's absence. Her grades, once a source of pride, plummeted as the world around her lost its vibrancy. The whispers from her classmates, laced with a morbid curiosity about the "rape" that never was, served as constant reminders of the horrific night. Sister Maria, a silent observer of Nyokabi's internal storm, became her anchor in this tempestuous sea of emotions.

One afternoon, Sister Maria, her gaze etched with concern, summoned Nyokabi to her office. The once lively space now felt suffocating, the weight of unspoken expectations hung heavy in the air.

"Nyokabi," Sister Maria began gently, "your final term grades are a cause for concern. I understand this isn't the easiest time for you, but..."

She hesitated, searching for the right words, and said, "The opportunity to study in the United States is still within your grasp. A few other students are leaving in less than a month, and you were meant to be on that plane with them."

Nyokabi stared vacantly at Sister Maria, the weight of the world pressing down on her. "I don't know if I have it in me," she mumbled, her voice barely a whisper.

Sister Maria placed a comforting hand on hers and said, "You do, Nyokabi, and you will. Githinji knew the risks when he chose to fight for Kenya's freedom. His absence shouldn't extinguish the flame of your potential. You can honor his memory by continuing your fight in your way, for your country, for yourself, and him. He can no longer fight, but if he were here, wouldn't he want you to keep moving forward?"

Nyokabi's carefully constructed dam crumbled, tears cascading down her cheeks. "But he didn't die fighting," she choked, the guilt gnawing at her. "He died because of me."

Sister Maria's brow furrowed in concern. "What do you mean, child?"

Taking a shuddering breath, Nyokabi poured out her heart. "He heard something, but I distracted him. If only I hadn't..." Her voice trailed off, the weight of the "what ifs" threatening to consume her.

"Nyokabi, there's no room for blame here," Sister Maria said firmly, her voice laced with compassion. "There was no way you could have foreseen what happened. He too made a choice, a choice to lower his guard. It was a tragic series of unfortunate events, but it wasn't your fault or his."

Nyokabi clung to Sister Maria's words, a lifeline in the churning sea of grief. The weight of guilt remained, a dull ache in her chest, but a flicker of understanding sparked within her. Githinji wouldn't have wanted her to be consumed by self-blame. He would have wanted her to fight, to live, to carry forward the torch of their shared dreams.

A flicker of hope flickered in Nyokabi's eyes. She said, "Sister Maria. I need time. There's no way I can be ready to leave Kenya next month."

Sister Maria nodded in understanding. "Of course, child. Grief takes its own time. Let's aim for a September start instead. We'll work on getting you on a plane in August."

A spark of determination, however faint, flickered across Nyokabi's face. "What about my studies?"

"Well," Sister Maria said, a gentle smile gracing her lips, "the last time we spoke, you were set on anthropology. I think you finally decided to pursue law?"

Nyokabi pondered for a moment, the wheels in her mind turning slowly. "Actually," she admitted, "I think I must pursue law now."

Sister Maria's smile widened. "Excellent choice! Justice needs strong voices like yours. We'll ensure you have all the resources you need to prepare for the repeat final exams."

Nyokabi managed a faint smile in return. It wasn't much, but it was a start, a fragile bud pushing through the cracked pavement of grief.

"There's another issue, Sister Maria," she confessed, her voice barely a whisper. "I don't know how to face my family. They'll want to talk about the 'rape,' and I..." Her voice trailed off, choked by unshed tears.

Sister Maria placed a comforting hand on hers. "Your parents love and respect Sister Madonna. Would you feel more comfortable if she accompanied you to tell them?"

Nyokabi's brow furrowed in thought. "Yes," she admitted, "that might be helpful. But I'm worried my father, especially, won't want to let me go so far away after all this."

A reassuring smile played on Sister Maria's lips. "He won't stop you once he understands the truth. Let's plan a trip home with Sister Madonna to explain everything. Together, we'll navigate this conversation as a team."

A sliver of light pierced the darkness within Nyokabi. The road to healing would be long and arduous, but with Sister Maria's unwavering support and the nascent flame of purpose flickering within her, she knew she wasn't alone. With time, she would learn to carry Githinji's memory not as a burden, but as a source of strength, a reminder to fight for their dreams, for her future, and a brighter Kenya.

Part 2
Chapter 26

The journey back home to talk to her parents felt different. Sister Madonna's gentle presence eased the tension, and Nyokabi found solace in open communication. Her parents, though devastated by Githinji and Njuguna's deaths, surprised her with their understanding. Their love, a constant throughout her life, provided a much-needed anchor. Her mother, ever the pillar of strength, had held Mama Njuguna through her own grief after confirmation of losing both her children.

The departure for the United States was a whirlwind of emotions. Excitement for this new chapter, a nervous flutter in her stomach at the prospect of such a radical change, and a deep, underlying grief for Githinji. Still, his memory fueled a newfound determination. He didn't want her to be consumed by sorrow, but to embrace this opportunity, to learn, to grow, and perhaps, one day, to fight for justice in her own way.

As the plane soared into the clouds, Kenya shrinking into a distant memory, Nyokabi took a deep breath. The future stretched before her, an uncharted map. The dormitory life, the new people, and the unfamiliar culture. It all felt daunting, yet exhilarating. But this time, she wouldn't face it alone. Sister

Maria trusted a nun she had known for years. She would be a beacon of support in a foreign land.

With a newfound sense of purpose and a heart brimming with hope, Nyokabi braced herself. This was a new beginning, a chance to honor Githinji's memory, a chance to build a future for herself, and a chance to contribute to the dream of a free Kenya, even from afar. The journey would be challenging, but with each step forward, she carried the weight of her grief, the love for her family and friends, and the burning embers of Githinji's spirit, all propelling her forward.

La Guardia International Airport bustled with a cacophony of sounds and sights, a stark contrast to the familiar sights and sounds of home. Nyokabi emerged from the arrivals gate, a lone person of color in a sea of unfamiliar faces. Then, amidst the throng, she spotted a welcoming smile and a familiar veil.

A nun, different from the ones at her school, stood there holding a placard with her name in bold letters. This nun, Sister Marie Claire, wore a more modern outfit, a sweater, and skirt paired with a veil in a contrasting color. Curiosity flickered in Nyokabi's eyes, but respect for her new guardian angel kept her from asking about the difference in attire.

"Hello Nyokabi," Sister Marie Claire greeted her, her voice warm and inviting. "I presume you're Sister Maria's student? Welcome to the United States!"

Nyokabi offered a small smile in return, relief washing over her. "Yes, Sister. Thank you for coming to meet me."

Sister Marie Claire's smile widened. "Consider it my pleasure. Sister Maria entrusted you to my care, and I take that very seriously. Think of me as your guide here. I'll take you to the university and introduce you to some people who can show you the ropes."

Nyokabi's heart swelled with gratitude. Sister Marie Claire's easy demeanor and genuine concern put her at ease. Here, in this strange new land, a familiar kindness bloomed, a promise of support and guidance. With a silent nod, Nyokabi knew she wouldn't face this new chapter alone. Sister Marie Claire, a beacon of hope in a foreign land, had begun to weave herself into the tapestry of Nyokabi's future. The journey ahead might be daunting, but with Sister Marie Claire by her side, Nyokabi felt a spark of courage ignite within her.

"Howard University is a prestigious institution. You must be very proud of yourself for getting accepted!" Sister Marie Claire stated. Howard University, the name resonated with an air of distinction, a legacy that both thrilled and daunted her.

Sister Marie Claire's unwavering faith, however, was infectious. "Howard University," she declared, a hint of pride coloring her voice, "is a prestigious institution, an ideal place to embark on your legal studies. I have no doubt you'll flourish there and forge strong friendships."

Nyokabi digested this revelation, a spark of resolve replacing the initial astonishment. Law school, a path that once seemed like a distant dream now stood before her as a tangible possibility. "Thank you, Sister," she responded, her voice imbued with a newfound conviction.

"Now then," Sister Marie Claire continued, a mischievous twinkle in her eyes, "tonight won't be spent sequestered within the confines of a convent. You need to build a support system here, to connect with people. We'll be staying with a friend this evening, and tomorrow morning, we'll set off for Washington D.C."

The prospect of meeting new faces, potential confidantes, and companions, soothed some of Nyokabi's anxieties. A network, Sister Marie Claire had emphasized. The word whispered of a sense of belonging, of a safety net in this foreign land. With a grateful smile, Nyokabi settled into the passenger seat, eager to embark on the next phase of her odyssey. The path ahead might be long and winding, but with Sister Marie Claire as her compass and a network of connections waiting to be formed, Nyokabi felt a surge of optimism for what the future held.

Chapter 27

It did not take Nyokabi a long time to settle into her college life. She had a full schedule and she needed to stay busy to focus and just go through the motions and settle into a routine. One day in class, there was a class discussion regarding human thinking how a mob can influence one's thought process, and how human beings can change their thinking because their yearning for acceptance supersedes their need to be right.

The discussion continued until one of the students stood up and said, "I disagree. I do not believe it is in human nature to conform, I know many people who do not follow the majority but prefer to stand out and speak out against injustice even if it goes against the majority of people around them."

Nyokabi had been quiet listening to the conversation until now. She stood up looked the other student in the eye and said, "I do not think you understand the prompt. The prompt is to help us understand why people follow the majority instead of standing on their own.

"And I am saying that is not inherent to human nature. It may be a trait in some but not all. I think most people prefer to be part of a group and watch how people behave in certain situations to know how to behave. They do not go to a place and try to impose their thoughts on the locals."

"Oh! Is that what the colonialists did in Kenya?" the student said.

Nyokabi felt a fire burning in her. That statement had hit too close to home. She yelled, "It is what the slaves did when they came here!"

"Okay, I think we can call it a day," the professor interjected. "Your assignments are to write a 500-word essay regarding human conformity." He concluded. "Devon and Nyokabi, please stay after class."

Devon was staring at Nyokabi and Nyokabi was glaring back at him. Nyokabi's world had shrunk to a tunnel vision of anger. The carefully constructed world of textbooks and lectures dissolved, replaced by the stark reality of her homeland's struggle. As the professor dismissed the class, Devon lingered, his gaze flickering between defiance and something akin to apology.

The professor, sensing the simmering tension, addressed them both. "Devon," he said, his voice calm but firm, "your point about nonconformity was valid, but the historical context you used was insensitive. There's a time and place for everything, and a classroom discussion isn't the platform for such volatile comparisons."

Devon mumbled an apology, his bravado shrinking under the weight of the professor's words.

Nyokabi, however, remained frozen in her silent fury. The professor, his gaze softening with understanding, turned to her.

"Nyokabi," he said gently, "your reaction is understandable. Devon's comment was insensitive, but using anger as a weapon won't foster productive dialogue. Your response was equally hurtful. Perhaps you can use this fire within you to fuel your essay. Write about conformity, yes, but also about the courage it takes to stand against the tide, to speak your truth even when it's uncomfortable."

His words resonated with Nyokabi. The anger began to recede, replaced by a flicker of determination. Githinji's memory, a constant presence in her heart, fueled a renewed sense of purpose. This wasn't just about an academic debate; it was about using her voice, about honoring the sacrifices made for her freedom to speak.

Looking at Devon, she saw not an adversary, but an opportunity. Maybe, through open dialogue, she could bridge the gap in understanding. With a nod, she acknowledged the professor's words. "Thank you, Professor," she said, her voice hoarse but resolute. "I think we both have a lot to learn from this."

"How about you both learn from each other; learn about the experience of the descendants of slaves and Devon you can learn about the experience of colonialism firsthand from Nyokabi. I think that will enrich the class discussions."

Nyokabi retreated into a self-imposed exile, determined to avoid Devon at all costs. His ability to trigger her raw emotions with a single, insensitive remark was a constant source of irritation. She religiously avoided eye contact in class, her lips sealed shut during discussions. The semester crawled by, each day a small victory in her silent war of attrition.

As the final exam loomed, a sliver of hope bloomed because the semester's end meant no more Devon. He was a senior taking this class as an elective. She fervently prayed their paths wouldn't cross again in the upcoming semester.

Chapter 28

Stepping into the new semester lecture hall, Nyokabi felt a wave of relief wash over her. The circular rows, rising towards the back, offered a fresh start. She settled near the front, leaving a buffer of empty seats to her right. As a group of friends jostled past, their chatter a prelude to an inevitable class-long conversation, Nyokabi made a split-second decision. She wasn't in the mood for friendly distractions. Standing up, she scanned the higher rows, spotting a lone student engrossed in a book. A sense of peace settled over her as she settled into the adjacent seat.

"I see I can't escape you," a voice broke the quiet, sending a shiver down Nyokabi's spine. She looked up to find Devon, his expression a mix of confusion and something akin to hurt.

"Ugh, I can move," she stammered, the urge to flee warring with a newfound desire to understand.

"Why?" Devon persisted. "I've tried apologizing. Those remarks in class, they weren't personal."

Nyokabi locked eyes with him for the first time since their confrontation. Shame prickled at her conscience. Her reaction had been raw, fueled by years of colonial scars. And her response, the flippant "slaves" comment—it wasn't fair either.

"Your comment was insensitive," she admitted, her voice barely a whisper. "We're still fighting for our independence, for a voice. Your people are free."

"See, that's where you're wrong," Devon countered, his voice low and intense. "We're not free. Not truly. Systemic racism, segregation, police brutality—these are the chains that bind us still. Black people are killed here, indiscriminately, for simply existing."

Nyokabi's anger softened, replaced by a flicker of recognition. The fire in Devon's eyes mirrored the same burning passion she'd seen in Githinji. Perhaps, beneath the initial hostility, there was a shared understanding, a common thread of struggle woven into the fabric of their experiences.

"I am sorry, for what I said and for taking so long to apologize," Nyokabi said.

Devon smiled. "I know." He said with a chuckle. A hesitant truce settled between Nyokabi and Devon, marked by her apology. Devon's responding chuckle, devoid of malice, held a hint of something unexpected—understanding. The professor's arrival, a welcome interruption, forced them to turn their attention to the lecture. Yet, as Nyokabi settled into her seat, a strange sensation washed over her.

For the first time, she consciously lowered her guard. The constant vigilance, the coiled tension within her, began to ease. A nascent thought, a tentative possibility, bloomed in her mind - friendship with Devon. Perhaps, through open dialogue, they could bridge the chasm of cultural experiences, forge a connection built on shared struggles. The idea captivated her, and she found herself stealing glances at Devon throughout the class, his form outlined against the backdrop of the lecture hall.

A pang of guilt, sharp and sudden, pierced through her newfound curiosity. It had been a year since Githinji's death, a year etched in the raw ache of grief. And yet, here she was, the memory of him dimmed by the spark of a new connection. Shame gnawed at her. Was she forgetting him so easily? Was this a betrayal of his love, his sacrifice?

A hesitant smile tugged at Nyokabi's lips as Devon offered to walk her back. The weight of her internal conflict remained, but the easy camaraderie in his voice, the absence of animosity, was disarming. She nodded, gathering her belongings with a mumbled thanks as he took the books from her hands.

Lost in thought, Nyokabi barely registered Devon's next move. His arm, a gentle weight on her shoulder, sent a jolt through her. Surprise flickered across her face, quickly followed by a hesitant smile.

"So," Devon chuckled, his voice warm, "who do I have to fight off to get this escort duty every day?"

The question, laced with a playful challenge, startled her out of her introspection. A genuine smile bloomed on her face, erasing the shadows of guilt and doubt. She playfully bumped her shoulder against his.

"Oh, you'll have to work hard for that information," she teased, relishing the unfamiliar lightness in her heart. "Maybe a semester's worth of good behavior will earn you the right to know."

Devon's grin widened. "Challenge accepted. But tell you what," he continued, his voice dropping a touch, "how about we ditch the dorms for a bit? I have a ton of questions for you, and the library just doesn't seem like the right atmosphere."

Nyokabi's eyes sparkled with newfound curiosity. "Coffee?" she offered, the question hanging in the air.

"Coffee sounds perfect," Devon replied, his smile mirroring hers. "So much to learn, so little time. Consider this the official start of our mutual interrogation."

Laughter bubbled up from Nyokabi's chest, a sound both foreign and exhilarating. Maybe, just maybe, friendship with Devon wasn't a betrayal of the past, but a bridge to a future filled with understanding, shared struggles, and perhaps, even healing.

Chapter 29

They sat at a corner booth away from the hustle and bustle of the people coming in and out of the coffee shop. It was conveniently placed close to the library and the majority of customers who came in were students from Howard.

"Tell me about yourself. Who is Nyokabi?"

"There are multiple layers to me. What do you want to know."

"Tell me about your family. Your brothers, sisters, are you the eldest?"

Nyokabi took a deep breath in. "How much time do you have?"

Devon smiled and settled in, signaling to her that he was in no hurry.

"Well, I have a total of fifteen brothers and sisters.

"Fifteen siblings!" Devon exclaimed, eyes wide with a mix of awe and amusement. "That's a whole army right there."

Nyokabi chuckled, a comfortable warmth spreading through her. "Well, not quite an army," she admitted, "but definitely a lively bunch. Only Mburu, my younger brother, is from my mother. The rest are stepbrothers and sisters."

"Your father has several wives, huh?" Devon raised an eyebrow. "That's a big family to support."

"It is," Nyokabi acknowledged. "Some of my brothers work in Nairobi, and Wanjau is almost done with his studies at Makerere University. My sisters are mostly married with children already. I guess I'm the odd one out, the one who ended up with the nuns and now studying abroad."

Devon leaned forward, genuine curiosity sparkling in his eyes. "Hold on, nuns? You lived in a convent? Why's that?"

Nyokabi took a sip of her coffee, the memory bittersweet. "It was safer and easier for me after...well, after things got difficult at home. Sister Madonna loved and mentored me like her own."

He nodded slowly, understanding dawning on his face. "Whoa, that's intense. Didn't you miss out on having a normal family life with your siblings?"

Nyokabi shook her head. "Not really. I saw them often, and I'm very close to my parents, and also my little brother." A flicker of sadness crossed her eyes, a fleeting tribute to the life that could have been.

"You know," Devon said, his voice gentle, "family comes in all shapes and sizes. Maybe the nuns and Sister Madonna were part of your family too, in their own way."

Nyokabi considered his words, their truth resonating deep within her. A grateful smile touched her lips. "You're right, Devon. Maybe they were."

The conversation flowed easily between them, a comfortable exchange of stories and experiences that chipped away at the remaining walls Nyokabi had built around her heart.

Curiosity flickered in her eyes. "What about you, Devon? What's your family like?"

He took a thoughtful sip of his coffee. "Compared to yours, mine seems rather ordinary, I suppose. Dad works as an elevator operator, and Mom cleans houses here and there. But they're the hardest-working people I know. Sacrificed everything to give me a good shot at life, always pushed me to chase my dreams."

A spark of understanding ignited in Nyokabi's eyes. "That's why we're both here, then," she said, the echo of shared ambition in her voice. "Law school. Why law, though?"

Devon leaned back in his chair, a determined glint in his eyes. "I've always seen injustice all around me. People getting pushed around, and treated unfairly just because of the color of their skin, and their background. Law seems like a way to fight for what's right, to level the playing field. What about you, Nyokabi?"

Nyokabi's gaze drifted out the window for a moment, her mind traveling back to her homeland. "In Kenya, we fight for our freedom, our voice. But the fight isn't over. Law seems like a way to continue that fight, even here. Sister Maria, the one who helped me get here, she saw that fire in me."

She explained how Sister Maria had intervened, ensuring she wouldn't be left behind after her ordeal. The weight of gratitude hung heavy in her voice. "Without her, I wouldn't be here, wouldn't have this chance."

A hesitant silence fell between Nyokabi and Devon. While their conversation flowed easily, a part of Nyokabi remained guarded. The memory of Githinji, a love too precious and painful to share, held her back from complete openness.

Curiosity, however, gnawed at her. She yearned to know more about Devon, about his experiences with love. But how to ask without venturing into territory too personal?

"So," she began, her voice tentative, "what's the dating scene like here in the US?"

Devon shifted uncomfortably in his seat, a flicker of something akin to shyness crossing his features. "Well," he admitted, scratching the back of his neck, "I won't deny I've had a few girlfriends. College life, especially being so far from home, comes with a certain kind of freedom, a chance to explore things differently."

Nyokabi let out a nervous laugh, the word "explore" leaving a hollow taste in her mouth. "Oh! Kiombeni!" she blurted out, a cultural reference tumbling out unexpectedly.

"Kiombeni?" Devon furrowed his brow, completely lost.

"It's a name we give to boys who attract a lot of girls during initiation ceremonies back home," Nyokabi explained, a forced smile playing on her lips. "Sometimes, a single boy could have as many as fifty girls chasing after him. They call him Kiombeni, a heartbreaker."

Devon's eyes widened in surprise. "Whoa! That's definitely not me," he declared with a chuckle. "Actually, I'm more of a serial monogamist, you could say." He winked at her, trying to lighten the mood.

"Serial monogamist?" Nyokabi echoed, a sliver of curiosity pushing aside her discomfort. "What's that?"

"It means I tend to be in committed relationships, one after the other," Devon explained. "Not the Kiombeni way, definitely not!"

A new thread of conversation emerged; a bridge built on cultural exchange. Nyokabi, emboldened by Devon's genuine interest, decided to elaborate on the concept of initiation ceremonies. She described the rituals, the guided exploration of intimacy, and the emphasis on healthy sexual maturity under the watchful eyes of elders.

As Devon listened, rapt attention replacing his initial surprise, a flicker of understanding passed between them. Perhaps, in this exchange of experiences, they were not just building a friendship, but chipping away at the walls of prejudice, one conversation at a time.

The friendly chime of the cafe door signaled their approaching departure. "We'll be closing in five minutes," the waitress chirped, peering at their table.

Devon glanced out the window, surprised to see the sky ablaze with the hues of sunset. "Goodness, it is late!" he exclaimed. "How did that happen?"

Nyokabi echoed his sentiment, mirroring his surprised gaze. She couldn't recall the last time hours had melted away like spilled coffee, consumed by the conversation that flowed effortlessly.

"So," she finally murmured, a touch of amusement in her voice, "you don't usually spend hours lost in conversation like this?"

He shook his head, a sheepish grin tugging at his lips. "Never. Honestly, I've never sat with anyone, girl or otherwise, and just talked for hours like this."

Her own lips curved into a smile. "I guess both of us had a first today, then," she replied.

Then, a playful note crept into his voice. "Are you trying to tell me you've never had a guy give you his undivided attention like this? Hard to believe."

Nyokabi's smile faltered. The question hung heavy in the air, a challenge she couldn't answer without revealing the carefully guarded secret of Githinji.

The shift in her demeanor didn't escape Devon's notice. His brow furrowed in concern, and he quickly reached for her backpack, placing it on his shoulder. "Let's head back," he suggested, his voice a touch softer.

The walk back to the dorm was shrouded in comfortable silence. Reaching the entrance, Devon offered her backpack with a concerned expression. "Here," he murmured, shoving his hands into his pockets. "I wouldn't want you to get into trouble with your boyfriend."

Startled, Nyokabi met his gaze. "I don't have a boyfriend," she blurted out, a tremor in her voice. "I had someone, but..." She choked back a sob, tears threatening to spill over.

Understanding dawned on Devon's face. "Hey," he said gently, "you don't have to talk about it if you're not ready." Without warning, he pulled her into a warm embrace, the gesture more comforting than romantic. He placed a soft kiss on her forehead. "Go inside," he said, his voice low. "I just need to see you safely in."

The sudden display of tenderness, so reminiscent of Githinji's embraces, left Nyokabi breathless. Tears sprung to her eyes, blurring her vision. With a mumbled "thank you," she turned and ran into the dorm, leaving a bewildered yet strangely hopeful Devon standing on the steps. The weight of her confession hung heavy in the air, a silent promise to share her story when she was ready, and a glimmer of a future friendship, perhaps even something more, blossoming in its wake.

Chapter 30

Nyokabi felt a hollowness settle in her stomach as the day unfolded without a glimpse of Devon. Senior year kept him swamped – deadlines looming, presentations piling up – a stark contrast to her own lighter junior schedule. She found herself glancing around her classrooms with a frequency bordering on obsession, a nervous flutter in her chest whenever a familiar voice echoed down the hallway.

Guilt gnawed at her. The memory of her tearful outburst, raw and unexpected, played on repeat in her mind. Had she scared him away? Was their burgeoning friendship, that unexpected bridge they were building, already crumbling?

Across campus, in the library's labyrinthine silence, Devon grappled with his own anxieties. Nyokabi's teary confession, a glimpse into a past shrouded in pain, had left him shaken. The weight of her unspoken story hung heavy, urging him to tread carefully. He buried himself in research, burying his own uncertainty beneath mountains of textbooks, highlighting passages with a fervor that belied his focus.

Finally, as Nyokabi's last class ended, she decided to seek solace in the familiar haven of the library. The promise of losing herself in another world, or another time, held a certain appeal. She browsed the towering shelves, her fingers trailing along the spines of American history books.

Suddenly, a familiar voice broke through the hushed silence. Looking up, Nyokabi met Devon's gaze. A hesitant smile played on his lips; a secret shared in the blink of an eye. His voice, when he spoke, was barely a whisper.

"American History?" he queried, a playful lilt in his voice.

A genuine smile bloomed on Nyokabi's face, erasing the shadows of doubt that had lingered. "Someone sparked my curiosity," she replied, the playful banter echoing their newfound connection.

Their eyes locked for a beat, a silent exchange that transcended words. Devon cleared his throat, breaking the comfortable silence.

"Well," he began, running a hand through his afro. "I've got a little more to finish up on these assignments. Want to keep me company while I study?"

Nyokabi felt a warmth bloom in her chest. Seeing him seek her company, even if for quiet study, filled a void she hadn't realized existed. "Sure," she replied, her voice barely above a whisper. "I was just about to head back with these books anyway. Studying here wouldn't be a bad idea."

Devon shuffled his belongings to make space, and they settled into a happy silence, each engrossed in their own world. Hours melted away, punctuated only by the occasional rustle of turning pages and the quiet hum of the library overhead.

Just as the afternoon light began to dim, Devon finally snapped his textbooks shut. He turned to Nyokabi, a smile playing on his lips. Studying seemed to have faded from his mind.

"You know," he murmured, his voice low and warm, "you're really beautiful."

Nyokabi's cheeks flushed. This wasn't something she was used to, compliments on her appearance taking her by surprise. She fidgeted with a corner of her blouse, unsure of how to respond.

Seeing her hesitation, Devon chuckled softly. "Did I catch you off guard there?" he asked, his voice gentle.

Before Nyokabi could form a reply, his gaze shifted. "Speaking of catching you," he continued, changing the subject with a hint of amusement, "have you eaten anything since lunch?"

Nyokabi shook her head. "Not really. I usually have tea around four."

"Tea!" Devon exclaimed, a playful grin spreading across his face. "You really are a queen, aren't you?"

Nyokabi couldn't help but laugh at his teasing. As they gathered their belongings and exited the library, a flicker of something new sparked between them.

"So," Devon leaned in conspiratorially, "how about some dinner? My treat, of course."

"I do have some food in the dorm..." Nyokabi began, her voice trailing off.

"No arguments," Devon declared, his smile unwavering. "Tonight, dinner is on me. Consider it a way to apologize for all those history books monopolizing my attention."

Part of Nyokabi wanted to protest, to insist on some independence. But another, deeper part, recognized a different motive behind his invitation. Perhaps it was his way of ensuring she wouldn't disappear again, of forging a stronger connection. Confused by this strange mix of emotions, Nyokabi found herself following him, a mixture of trepidation and excitement bubbling in her stomach.

"Okay," she finally agreed, a hint of a smile peeking through. "Where are we going?"

Devon winked. "Follow me," he said, a mischievous glint in his eye. "I have a place in mind that will show you a different side of American life."

With that, he set off with a confident stride, leaving Nyokabi to wonder where this unexpected turn of events might lead.

Chapter 31

The warmth of the small restaurant enveloped them as Devon ushered Nyokabi through the door. A woman behind the counter, her face creased with a welcoming smile, greeted Devon like a beloved son.

"How you been, honey?" she boomed, her voice rich and Southern. "Ain't seen you in a week."

"School's kicking my butt, Ms. Davis," Devon replied with a chuckle. "Gotta buckle down and crush the LSATs for grad school."

"That's right! Ain't that the truth?" Ms. Davis chuckled, her gaze then flickering to Nyokabi. "And who might this beautiful young lady be?"

"This is Nyokabi," Devon announced, placing a hand on Nyokabi's back in a friendly gesture. "We're good friends."

Ms. Davis's eyebrows shot up in a playful manner. "Mm-hm," she drawled, her gaze lingering on their hands brushing. "Well, you better treat her right, young man. She seems like a lovely young lady."

"Oh, I plan on it," Devon assured her, his voice warm. "Starting with a proper meal." He turned to Nyokabi, a hint of amusement sparkling in his eyes. "This is Ms. Davis, Nyokabi. She and Mr. Davis practically raised me on their good cooking since freshman year."

Ms. Davis, a robust woman with an infectious smile, reached across the counter to shake Nyokabi's hand that was already stretched out. "Proper, that's right, honey," she declared, her voice booming. "And Devon, you hear me? You be good to this one. Now, y'all go on and have a seat. I'll whip up a plate of somethin' special—some good ol' Southern comfort food to fill your bellies."

A wave of shyness washed over Nyokabi as Ms. Davis's warm gaze lingered on them a moment too long, particularly when she noticed the woman focusing on their intertwined hands.

"Why was she looking at us like that?" Nyokabi ventured, attempting to mask her self-consciousness.

"Maybe because I was holding your hand," Devon replied with a teasing smile. "What about it?"

"In my culture," Nyokabi explained hesitantly, "holding hands doesn't necessarily have a romantic meaning. It's common to hold hands with a sibling or a close friend."

A flicker of understanding crossed Devon's face. "Oh, I see," he said, a thoughtful pause breaking the silence. "Does that bother you now that you know what it means here?"

Nyokabi met his gaze, a wry smile playing on her lips. To her own surprise, she found herself whispering, "No."

The simple word hung in the air, a silent confession that sent a thrill coursing through Devon. Perhaps, just perhaps, their friendship was blossoming into something more, a connection that transcended cultural boundaries, fueled by shared experiences and a burgeoning sense of care.

"Now tell me all I need to know about you and your culture," Devon said. A look of genuine interest washed over

Devon's face as Nyokabi began to explain her culture's intricate social structure. The concept of age and status being so deeply intertwined fascinated him.

"So, there are these different stages of life, marked by rituals like initiation," he summarized, eager to ensure he understood correctly. "Each stage comes with increased respect and responsibility within the community."

Nyokabi nodded, a thoughtful expression on her face. "Exactly," she confirmed. "It's about recognizing your place in the larger circle of life, your contribution to the family and society as a whole."

"That's beautiful," Devon murmured, genuinely touched by the emphasis on community and respect for elders. "It's so different from the individualistic focus here in the US."

Nyokabi smiled. "There are pros and cons to every system, I suppose," she replied diplomatically. "But in my culture, there's always a strong sense of belonging, of knowing you're part of something bigger than yourself."

"And where does, say, holding hands fit into all this?" Devon asked, a playful glint in his eyes.

Nyokabi chuckled, a blush creeping up her cheeks. "As I said, holding hands doesn't have a specific romantic connotation back home. It's more about physical closeness, showing affection or support."

Devon feigned mock seriousness. "Oh, no," he drawled, a playful smile tugging at his lips. "Then it seems I've been sending some seriously mixed signals here."

Nyokabi's heart fluttered in her chest. She wasn't sure if he was teasing or not, but the playful banter sent a wave of warmth through her.

"Perhaps," she conceded, a playful smile mirroring his own. "But then again, maybe some signals are universal."

Their conversation continued to flow easily, Devon peppering her with questions about her life in Kenya, his genuine interest evident in his attentive gaze. Nyokabi, in turn, found herself drawn to his open-mindedness, his eagerness to understand a world so different from his own.

As Ms. Davis arrived with their steaming plates of Southern comfort food, an easy silence settled between them, a relaxing silence brimming with unspoken possibilities.

The conversation took a sharp turn as Nyokabi delved into the complexities of courtship and intimacy in Kikuyu culture. Devon listened intently, his initial lighthearted question morphing into a moment of genuine cultural exchange.

Nyokabi explained the concept of Ngweko, the supervised premarital intimacy practiced during initiation ceremonies. A wave of heat flushed over her cheeks as she spoke, the weight of tradition and past experiences battling within her.

"So, sex was a healthy part of growing up?" Devon finally asked, his voice thoughtful.

Nyokabi nodded hesitantly. "In a way, yes. It was about guided exploration, about learning your body and developing emotional bonds without the pressure of intercourse."

She then delved into the expectations surrounding marriage and sexuality within the Kikuyu community. The emphasis on virginity before marriage, the strictures against premarital intercourse, and the focus on procreation within marriage – it was a stark contrast to the casual nature of dating Devon described.

"Wow," Devon finally breathed, a mix of surprise and respect coloring his voice. "It's so different from how things are here. So much stricter."

Nyokabi shrugged, a touch of defensive creeping into her tone. "Different, yes," she said. "But it has its own kind of logic, a way of ensuring social order and family stability."

"I understand," Devon assured her, his voice gentle. "It's just... a lot to take in." He fell silent for a moment, his gaze flickering across her face. "Though," he continued, a hint of a smile playing on his lips, "I have to admit, the part about no 'exchange of bodily fluids' until after marriage... that's a pretty interesting concept."

Nyokabi couldn't help but laugh at his teasing, the tension breaking slightly. "Well," she countered playfully, "perhaps American dating culture could learn a thing or two about taking things a bit slower."

Despite the cultural differences they were exploring, a sense of connection bloomed between them. They were two souls navigating unfamiliar territory, their conversation a bridge between their worlds. The weight of Nyokabi's past remained unspoken, a silent undercurrent in their newfound understanding. But for now, they were content in the present moment, savoring the unexpected intimacy that their shared meal had fostered.

A flicker of vulnerability crossed Devon's face as he reached across the table. "So," he began, his voice soft, "can I see you tomorrow?"

Nyokabi felt a warmth bloom in her chest. The invitation, so simple yet meaningful, sent a thrill through her. "I have classes all day," she replied, "but I'm free after three thirty. I'll be at the library working on a paper."

"Perfect!" Devon beamed. "I'll be there after my classes too. We can study together, and maybe grab dinner again afterwards?"

Nyokabi couldn't help but smile. "Sounds like a plan," she agreed.

Devon, emboldened by her positive response, reached for his wallet to settle the bill. As he did, his hand brushed against hers. This time, when he held her hand, the sensation was different. A spark of electricity crackled between them; a silent language spoken through touch.

Walking her back to her dorm room, the air crackled with unspoken possibility. Reaching her door, Devon hesitated, a nervous energy radiating from him. He gently lifted her chin, his gaze searching hers. Before she could speak, he leaned in, his lips brushing softly against hers.

Nyokabi gasped, startled by the suddenness of it all. For a moment, she stood frozen, unsure how to react. A wave of emotions washed over her—surprise, confusion, a flicker of something deeper.

Sensing her hesitation, Devon pulled back immediately, a look of apology on his face. "I'm so sorry," he murmured, his voice filled with regret. "I shouldn't have done that. I didn't mean to make you uncomfortable."

Nyokabi searched his eyes, the sincerity in his gaze calming the storm of emotions within her. "It's not that," she whispered, her voice barely audible.

Taking a deep breath, she surprised herself by leaning back in, her voice a touch firmer. "Do it again," she said, her gaze steady.

A slow smile spread across Devon's face, his eyes sparkling with delight. This time, the kiss was different. It was slow, lingering, filled with a yearning that neither of them could deny. Time seemed to melt away as they lost themselves in the moment, the kiss a silent promise of what could be.

Finally, Devon pulled away, his voice husky with emotion. "Goodnight, Nyokabi," he whispered, his forehead resting against hers. "Go get some rest. I should probably head back too before I lose my head completely."

Nyokabi smiled at his playful words. The night, filled with unexpected revelations and a newfound closeness, had left her heart pounding. With a shy nod, she turned and entered her dorm, the taste of Devon's kiss lingering on her lips, a sweet reminder of the evening's unexpected turn.

Nyokabi walked back to her dorm, her mind a whirlwind of emotions. The kiss, her first ever, left a tingling sensation on her lips and a new warmth blooming in her chest. But tangled with this newfound joy was a knot of worry.

Devon's genuine interest, his respect for her boundaries, all of it fueled a desire in her to explore this connection further. Yet, the weight of her past, the ghost of Githinji, loomed large.

She realized the cultural explanation she'd provided might have painted an inaccurate picture. Devon might believe she was a virgin, based on the Kikuyu expectations of marriage. If this blossoming friendship, tinged with undeniable attraction, was to have a chance, she needed to tell him about Githinji.

A sliver of gratitude pierced her worry. Devon hadn't pushed things further after her reaction when he inquired about male interest. It spoke volumes about his character and his respect for her. But she knew his curiosity must be piqued.

Taking a deep breath, Nyokabi steeled herself. Honesty, she knew, was the only path forward. She had to find a way to share her story, to explain the complexities of her past, the love, and loss that had shaped her. It wouldn't be easy, but the possibility of a future with Devon, the warmth of his kiss, gave her the courage to face that challenge. She would find a way to navigate this new territory, to find peace with her past, and make room for the possibility of new love.

Chapter 32

The clock on the lecture room wall seemed to tick with agonizing slowness, each second stretching into an eternity. Finally, the class was over. With a newfound resolve propelling her forward, she hurried across campus, her destination clear - the library and Devon.

Pushing open the heavy oak doors, Nyokabi scanned the rows of studious figures. Her gaze quickly landed on Devon; his head bent intently over a textbook. A radiant smile blossomed on her face, chasing away the lingering anxieties of the day.

"Hello!" she announced, sliding into the chair next to him with a soft thud.

Devon's head snapped up, a brilliant smile replacing his focused frown. He leaned in, his lips brushing softly against hers in a sweet greeting. A familiar warmth fluttered in Nyokabi's stomach; a spark ignited by his touch.

"Hey, baby," Devon murmured, the endearment hanging in the air.

Nyokabi's smile faltered slightly. The term, while playful from Devon, felt unfamiliar on his lips. Public displays of affection weren't something she was accustomed to either, and "baby" held a different connotation coming from Ms. Davis, a term of maternal warmth.

"I guess that's a pet name?" she ventured, a hint of amusement dancing in her voice.

"Absolutely," Devon confirmed, winking.

"But then again, Ms. Davis called you 'baby' too, didn't she?" Nyokabi pressed.

Devon nodded. "Yes, but it feels different coming from her, you know?" he explained. "Like the affection of a family member."

Understanding dawned on Nyokabi's face. "Ah, I see," she said, a thoughtful expression settling on her features.

"Cultural differences, huh?" Devon asked.

Nyokabi chuckled. "Seems so. But enough about that," she added, eager to move on to the weightier matter on her mind. "I have something I need to tell you."

Devon's playful demeanor instantly shifted into one of concern. He straightened in his chair, his hand hovering over hers on the table. "What happened?" he asked, his voice laced with worry.

Taking a deep breath, Nyokabi met his gaze. "It's about my past," she began, her voice barely a whisper.

"Okay, let's walk to the dinner as we talk," Devon said.

They walked out of the library, she then proceeded to tell him about the Mau Mau uprising, Githinji's involvement, their secret meetings, and ultimately, his tragic death.

As she spoke, the world faded away, replaced by a vivid mental tapestry of the events she recounted. She poured out her heart, the raw emotions of the past year spilling forth in a torrent of honesty. When she finished, a heavy silence descended upon them, thick with unspoken thoughts and feelings.

"How long ago was that?" Devon finally asked, his voice quiet and gentle.

"A year," Nyokabi replied, her voice catching slightly.

Silence stretched once more, a tense quietude that seemed to press in on them. Nyokabi stole a glance at Devon, desperately trying to decipher the emotions swirling behind his eyes. His usual playful demeanor was gone, replaced by a thoughtful seriousness that sent a shiver down her spine.

She almost blurted out an apology, a reassurance that dinner wasn't necessary. But before she could voice her anxieties, Devon surprised her by placing his hand on her shoulder.

"I can eat in the dorm. We don't have to go to dinner," Nyokabi ventured.

A faint smile touched his lips. "I'm famished," he declared with a playful drawl, a hint of amusement dancing in his eyes. "Looks like Ms. Davis's delicious cooking will have to wait a bit longer. There's a fantastic burger joint down the street I've been wanting to try."

Nyokabi's heart sank. His attempt at humor, while sweet, did little to alleviate her growing unease. She yearned to understand what he was thinking, to know if her past had irrevocably altered his perception of her.

As if sensing her worry, Devon reached out and gently squeezed her hand. His touch, a silent language of reassurance, sent a wave of warmth through her.

"Let's go," he continued, his voice firm and steady. "I'm processing everything you told me. Give me a minute, okay? But trust me, the last thing I want is for you to leave right now."

Nyokabi felt a surge of relief washes over her. His words were a balm to her anxieties. They continued their walk in silence, his arm finding its way around her waist, a silent promise of support. The path ahead remained uncertain, but for now, the warmth of his touch and the quiet strength in his gaze offered a solace she desperately needed.

Chapter 33

They sat down to eat. The conversation took a sweet turn as they settled into their meal. Nyokabi, emboldened by her decision to share her past, surprised even herself.

"Not sure how I can compete with him," Devon began, a touch of self-doubt creeping into his voice. "There seems like there's no room for me after all he meant to you."

Nyokabi reached across the table, her touch warm and reassuring. "That's not true at all," she said softly. "You hold a very different, very special place in my heart. Remember, you were the one who received my first kiss."

As she spoke, she saw a weight lift from Devon's shoulders, a flicker of relief replacing his earlier apprehension. A genuine smile bloomed on his face, chasing away the shadows of doubt.

"Are you saying you like me?" he teased, a playful glint in his eyes.

Nyokabi returned the playful jab with a mock frown. Devon's laughter filled the air, a welcome melody to her ears. It was a sound that spoke volumes, a sound that eased the tension that had unknowingly built between them.

"There's no shame in admitting it, Nyokabi," he said, his voice laced with amusement. "I like you too. Why else would I be spending all this time with you, sharing meals and studying together?"

A more serious expression settled on Devon's face. He leaned forward, his voice dropping to a husky whisper. "But for real," he said, his gaze searching hers, "is there anything I need to worry about? Any past relationships back home that might complicate things?"

Nyokabi shook her head, a wave of relief washing over her. "No," she assured him, meeting his gaze with honesty. "There's no one else. Githinji will always hold a special place in my memories, but he's gone. And the truth is, I've already spent so much more time with you than I ever did with him."

Taking a deep breath, Nyokabi decided to fully embrace the moment. With a newfound confidence, she leaned in and surprised them both by initiating another kiss. This kiss was different, deeper, fueled by a growing sense of intimacy and a budding affection. When they finally pulled away, a contented silence settled between them, a silence thick with unspoken emotions.

"Just one question, though," Nyokabi said finally, a playful smile on her lips.

"Anything," Devon replied, his voice husky with unspoken desire.

"What about girlfriends here?" she countered, a playful jab.

Devon threw his head back and laughed, a rich, genuine sound that warmed Nyokabi's heart. "Don't you worry about a thing," he assured her, squeezing her hand gently. "You have absolutely nothing to worry about. Now, let's finish this delicious food, and then maybe we can take a walk and enjoy this beautiful evening together."

The weight of the past seemed to recede for a moment, replaced by the exhilarating promise of a future yet to be written. As they continued their meal, in silence, punctuated only by the clinking of silverware and the quiet hum of conversation around them. A fragile connection had bloomed, nurtured by honesty, vulnerability, and a spark of undeniable attraction. The road ahead might hold challenges, but for now, they were content to savor the present moment, hand in hand, hearts tentatively open to the possibilities that lay before them.

Three months flew by in a whirlwind of stolen glances, late-night study sessions, and a deepening connection between Nyokabi and Devon. Their cultural differences became a source of amusement and exploration, each learning new things about the other's world.

However, the ghost of Githinji hadn't entirely vanished. There were still days when a stray thought, a fleeting memory, particularly of his eyes in those final moments, would send a pang of grief through Nyokabi.

Finally, the day arrived when Devon invited her to his dorm room. The air crackled with unspoken desires, a culmination of three months of simmering tension. Self-control crumbled, and they surrendered to a passionate exploration of each other. Hours melted away in a haze of intimacy, leaving them both gloriously exhausted.

As Nyokabi lay nestled against Devon, a sliver of unease crept in. A silent question formed in her mind: could Githinji see her from some celestial plane? The thought felt intrusive, a betrayal of sorts.

Just then, Devon's voice broke the silence. "We should probably grab some food," he said, his voice husky with sleep. "You hungry?"

Nyokabi blinked, the unsettling thought momentarily banished. "Starving," she admitted with a small smile.

"Well then," Devon grinned, "in that case, why don't I go get some takeout? There's that great place around the corner I've been wanting to try. Relax, you look like you could use a rest. No one will bother you here."

Nyokabi hesitated. Spending the night felt like a significant step, a deeper level of commitment. But the warmth radiating from Devon, the feeling of safety and belonging, proved persuasive.

"Alright," she agreed, a shy smile gracing her lips.

Devon leaned down and brushed a soft kiss against her forehead. "Great. I'll be back in a jiffy."

With that, he slipped out of bed, leaving Nyokabi alone with her thoughts. The unease flickered again, but this time it was overshadowed by a new sensation - a burgeoning sense of hope for the future, a future she was ready to build with Devon, one delicious meal and stolen glance at a time.

The night deepened, after dinner, but Nyokabi's anxieties refused to settle. The joy of their earlier intimacy gave way to a gnawing worry about Devon's impending graduation and return to California.

"You'll be graduating soon, heading back to California," she said softly, a tremor in her voice.

Devon, nestled close beside her, turned to face her with a smile. "Are you worried you'll miss me?" he teased; his voice laced with amusement.

Nyokabi offered a dramatic sigh. "Oh, devastated," she exaggerated, forcing a smile.

"I am not going anywhere; I have grad school to keep me here. Speaking of which, I got accepted!"

"Wait, you did?" Nyokabi shot up, surprised delight coloring her features. "That's fantastic! Why didn't you tell me?"

"Well, I was just about to—" Devon began, but Nyokabi cut him off with another question.

"Do your parents know?"

"Actually," Devon admitted, a hint of nervousness creeping into his voice, "there's something I've been meaning to tell you." He took her hand in his, his touch warm and reassuring. "I wrote a letter to my parents a few weeks ago, telling them about us. I want you to come with me when I go tell them the good news."

Nyokabi's breath hitched. Back in Kenya, meeting the parents was a significant step, a gesture laden with the weight of commitment. "Devon," she began cautiously, "that's wonderful, but shouldn't we have discussed this first? Meeting your parents feels like a big deal."

"A big deal?" Devon echoed, a touch of confusion in his voice.

"Exactly," Nyokabi confirmed, a knot of worry tightening in her stomach. "Back home, introducing someone to your parents is practically a proposal. You wouldn't bring someone home unless you intended on marrying them."

A soft chuckle escaped Devon's lips. "Baby," he assured her, using his pet name for her, "if I were proposing, you'd know it. There'd be a ring, a romantic setting, the whole nine yards. Trust me."

Relief washed over Nyokabi, momentarily easing her anxieties. "So, what's the purpose of me meeting your parents then?" she asked, her voice calmer now.

"Just for them to meet the amazing woman I'm dating," Devon replied simply. "The woman who makes my heart skip a beat."

Nyokabi smiled at his sweet words. However, a sliver of doubt lingered.

"To be absolutely clear," she pressed, "this isn't some test to see if I'm 'marriage material'?"

Devon's brow furrowed. "Marriage material? Nyokabi, I plan on marrying you but that will be when we are both ready." After a pause, he looked in her eyes and said. "Well, are you ready?"

"Aren't we supposed to be focused on finishing school?" Nyokabi asked with a playful smile.

A grin spread across Devon's face. "Alright, alright," he conceded, pulling her closer. "Maybe someday, when we're both ready. But for now, I just want you to know this – I love you."

The words hung in the air, a weight of significance settling between them. It was the first time he'd uttered those three little words, and the sincerity in his voice sent a warmth blooming in Nyokabi's chest.

"I love you too, Devon," she whispered, her voice thick with emotion. "And you should know," she added, a shy smile gracing her lips, "this is the first time I've said it to anyone besides my family."

A comfortable silence descended upon them, a silence rich with unspoken emotions and a newfound understanding. The conversation had been unexpected, a tangled mess of cultural differences and unspoken assumptions. But in the end, they had managed to navigate it, emerging stronger and closer on the other side.

"Well, that was a strange conversation," Devon finally admitted with a chuckle, breaking the silence.

"But a necessary one," Nyokabi agreed, returning his smile. "I'm glad we cleared the air."

Devon leaned in and brushed a soft kiss against her lips. "So," he murmured, his voice husky with unspoken desire, "about California... are you still up for the adventure?"

Nyokabi hesitated for a moment, a playful glint in her eyes. "How many girlfriends have you brought home to meet your parents?" she teased.

Devon's smile faltered slightly. "Honestly? Two," he admitted, a hint of sheepishness in his voice. "But that was back in high school. You, Nyokabi, would be the first one!"

"Okay, I will go." Nyokabi said.

A wave of relief washed over Devon. He hadn't realized how much unspoken tension had built up between them. Now, with everything laid bare, a sense of lightness filled the air.

"California trip, huh?" he repeated, a grin splitting his face. "Sounds like a plan! We should probably start looking at flights."

Nyokabi leaned in, her eyes sparkling with amusement. "And maybe we should also brainstorm some fun activities. California has something for everyone, you know."

Their conversation shifted, morphing into an excited exchange of ideas for their upcoming trip. They listed must-see places, debated the merits of different beaches, and even tossed around the possibility of a road trip.

As the night wore on, the conversation turned more intimate. Laughter mingled with whispered secrets, and gentle touches spoke volumes. They rediscovered each other, not just as lovers, but as partners ready to navigate the exciting, and sometimes confusing, path of cross-cultural love.

With a content sigh, Nyokabi snuggled closer to Devon. "This night started with some bumps in the road," she murmured, her voice laced with sleepiness.

"But hey," Devon replied, nuzzling her, "at least we ended up on the same page. And maybe," he added with a wink, "we even got a sneak peek at some future road trip adventures."

Nyokabi chuckled, a soft, sleepy sound. "Maybe we did," she agreed, her eyelids drooping. "Now," she mumbled, her voice barely a whisper, "how about we continue exploring each other, California-style?"

A slow, seductive smile spread across Devon's face. "I thought you'd never ask," he whispered, and with that, they drifted off to sleep, tangled in each other's arms.

Chapter 34

Nyokabi had not heard from Sister Madonna for a while. Nyokabi also noticed that the last two letters she had written to her were unanswered. She started to worry. The only way she would find out what was going on with Sister Madonna was to ask about her in a letter to Sister Maria. She was also concerned because every time she needed to send a message to her parents, Sister Madonna delivered it.

She also desperately needed to know how her family was doing. She expressed these thoughts to Devon. Who encouraged her to write to sister Maria. That afternoon, she needed to travel to New Jersey. She wanted to know if Sister Marie Claire had heard anything from Kenya and if there was a way for her to communicate with Sister Maria outside of sending letters. Devon was happy to accompany her to New Jersey.

Sister Marie Claire was happy to welcome them. She also sent a telegram to Sister Maria. Who responded a few hours later that she had seen Sister Madonna a few weeks ago and Sister Madonna was diagnosed with stage four pancreatic cancer. She was not doing so well and they were all praying for her.

Nyokabi's heart sank as the news about Sister Madonna settled in. The silence from her letters, the fatigue she'd noticed

– it all clicked into place with horrifying clarity. Sister Madonna had cancer, and it was advanced.

Grief threatened to engulf Nyokabi. Sister Madonna had been a constant presence in her life, a source of comfort and guidance. The thought of losing her was a crushing blow. Tears welled up in her eyes, blurring the world around her.

Devon, sensing her distress, pulled her close, offering silent support. His presence was a grounding force in the storm of emotions swirling within her.

Taking a shaky breath, Nyokabi clung to a sliver of hope. Sister Maria had offered a lifeline – a way to stay connected, to send messages to her family and receive updates on Sister Madonna's condition. It wasn't ideal, but it was something.

Grateful for Devon's unwavering support, Nyokabi decided to focus on the positive. She would write to her family, express her love, and cherish the memories she had with Sister Madonna. She would hold onto hope for a miracle, but also prepare herself for the inevitable.

The news about Sister Madonna cast a long shadow over Nyokabi's life. The joy of her relationship with Devon was tempered by the looming loss. Yet, amidst the grief, there was also a newfound appreciation for the preciousness of life and the importance of cherishing loved ones, both present and absent.

Chapter 35

Excitement crackled in the air as Devon led Nyokabi up the familiar path to his childhood home. He'd meticulously planned this trip, ensuring every detail would create a wonderful experience for Nyokabi. As they arrived, a wave of warmth washed over Nyokabi – Devon's family greeted them with open arms and genuine smiles.

Nyokabi presented gifts to Devon's parents, a token of appreciation for their hospitality. When she addressed Devon's mom as "mama," a look of pure delight lit up her face.

"Oh, my goodness, she called me mama!" Devon's mom exclaimed; her voice thick with emotion.

Nyokabi, initially confused by the reaction, quickly understood. In her culture, addressing someone's parent as "mama" or "baba" was a sign of respect. Devon's mom was not expecting Nyokabi to address her like that. A warm smile bloomed on her face as Devon's mom pulled her into a tight embrace, followed by a kiss on the cheek.

"Come on, child, get inside! It's getting chilly out here," Devon's mom called out to Devon, who was bringing in their luggage.

A long hug ensued between Devon and his mom, her affection overflowing. Finally, with a lingering kiss on his cheek, she ushered them both into the house.

Despite the initial struggle with the African-American dialect, Nyokabi had grown accustomed to it. Her focus had shifted from deciphering accents to truly connecting with the people around her. Now, the different sounds simply added a unique melody to the conversations.

Devon's mom's voice, however, held a new surprise. "Show Nyiakabi up to your room, honey," she instructed Devon. "I imagine you two will be sharing since we'll have a full house this weekend." A slight chuckle escaped her lips as she attempted to pronounce Nyokabi's name."

Nyokabi couldn't hide a flicker of surprise. Sharing a room with Devon here, under his parents' roof – it was a gesture that held a deeper meaning in her culture.

A satisfied smile played on Devon's mom's lips. "Told you you'd like her," Devon whispered conspiratorially, his voice laced with pride.

"Hello there, young lady," boomed a warm voice. Nyokabi turned to see a man with a kind smile approaching them. He extended a hand in greeting.

"Hey Dad," Devon responded, pulling Nyokabi closer.

"You must be Nyiakabi," the man said, his gaze fixed on Nyokabi.

"Nyokabi, Dad," Devon corrected gently.

The man chuckled, a deep, rumbling sound. "No worries, I'll get it with a little practice. Now, make yourselves at home. Your cousins, aunts, and uncles are all itching to meet you."

Devon led Nyokabi towards his old bedroom, their fingers brushing playfully. They dropped their luggage on the bed, and before they could step away, Devon leaned in for a quick kiss. A wave of heat washed over Nyokabi, a delicious blend of nervousness and excitement.

As loud voices and laughter filtered in from downstairs, Devon grinned. "Family can be a bit overwhelming sometimes," he admitted.

Nyokabi, however, couldn't help but feel a surge of apprehension. "Wait a minute, Devon," she began hesitantly. "At home, sharing a room with someone, especially around family, is for married couples only. And there's a whole process for introductions – this is very different from what I'm used to."

Devon's smile softened. "Nyokabi," he said, his voice sincere, "bringing you home to meet everyone is a big deal for me. It means you're special. You're the one I want my family to know."

Nyokabi couldn't help but tease him playfully. "Oh, so there are other girls who aren't special?"

Devon's eyes widened in mock surprise. "Oh no, you caught me there," he admitted with a laugh. They shared a chuckle, the tension momentarily broken. Taking a deep breath, Nyokabi reached for his hand. "Alright," she said, a hint of a smile gracing her lips, "let's face the family." With Devon by her side, she felt a surge of courage. This cultural navigation might be uncharted territory, but she was ready to embrace it, one awkward introduction at a time.

As they stepped into the living room, a chorus of greetings erupted. A woman with sleek, straightened hair approached them, a wide smile plastered on her face.

"Look at this lovey-dovey couple!" she exclaimed, gesturing between Nyokabi and Devon. "All smiles and holding hands! So cute!"

"Nyokabi, this is Ashley, my cousin," Devon introduced her.

The evening unfolded in a flurry of introductions and curious questions. Everyone seemed eager to get to know Nyokabi – how she and Devon met, what attracted her to him, her overall impressions of America.

"So, how has your stay in the States been so far?" a kindly-looking relative inquired.

"It's been good, for the most part," Nyokabi replied cautiously.

Another relative leaned in, their voice laced with concern. "What do you mean, 'for the most part'? Have you already encountered some difficulties?"

Nyokabi hesitated, a flicker of discomfort crossing her features. Devon, sensing her unease, squeezed her hand gently. "It's okay, Nyokabi," he murmured. "You can tell them. Most of us have dealt with racism our entire lives, we understand."

Taking a deep breath, Nyokabi decided to be honest. "The first few months were challenging," she admitted. "I mostly kept to myself, only interacting with classmates for school projects. But there were some... unpleasant encounters."

Her voice grew quiet as she recounted some of the hurtful remarks she'd endured – the ignorant assumptions about Africa, the mocking of her accent. The room fell silent as she spoke, a collective sense of empathy washing over the family.

"And on top of that," she added, a hint of a smile gracing her lips as she glanced at Devon, "there are so many different accents in America! I was used to British English, but here it seems everyone has their own way of speaking. It's a lot to take in."

Despite the initial difficulties, Nyokabi's voice held a note of resilience. And as she finished her story, a wave of warmth filled the room. Laughter erupted, not at her expense, but in shared amusement at the absurdity of the comments she'd faced.

"Well," boomed a voice, breaking the tension, "that's just plain rude! But don't you worry, honey. We'll have you speaking American slang in no time."

Despite the initial awkwardness, she was beginning to feel a sense of belonging. Devon's family, with their warmth and understanding, was slowly becoming her own.

Chapter 36

Ashley's update regarding his hometown painted a grim picture of Devon's reality. The carefree days of childhood friendships were shadowed by the harsh realities of police brutality and racial profiling. Nyokabi, who hadn't witnessed such things firsthand, felt a growing sense of unease. Her apprehension wasn't lost on Devon, whose reassuring squeeze conveyed a silent message of understanding.

"Welcome to the real world," he murmured, his voice tinged with a sadness that belied his earlier cheer. "Things are different here than in the safe bubble of campus life."

The conversation shifted as Devon inquired about Richard, a childhood friend. Ashley's head shake and somber expression spoke volumes before she even spoke.

"Still living in the same old house," she began, her voice low. "His mom passed away last month. Heart attack, they say. Went to the hospital, waited for hours, then died in the waiting room. Never even saw a doctor." Her voice grew heavy with frustration. "They just don't believe us when we say we are in pain."

A wave of sympathy washed over Nyokabi. The story resonated with a deep sense of injustice. Here, life and healthcare seemed to be a gamble, weighted heavily by race and circumstance.

Devon's jaw clenched, and a flicker of anger sparked in his eyes. "I need to see him," he declared, his voice firm. "I have to go see Richard before I head back to school."

The weight of reality had settled upon them, casting a shadow over the initial excitement of the visit. Yet, amidst the concern, a newfound understanding bloomed between Nyokabi and Devon. They were about to embark on a journey together, a journey not just of love and cultural exchange, but of navigating a world where the color of your skin could impact every aspect of your life. And in that moment, they held onto each other, a silent promise to face whatever came their way, together.

After dinner, most of Devon's family started leaving and soon there were just a few people left. "We need to go get some rest. We have had a long day and we are still on East Coast time," Devon said.

Nyokabi's heartfelt sigh hung heavy in the air. The initial excitement of the visit had given way to a sobering realization. As they walked hand-in-hand toward Devon's room, the weight of the world seemed to settle on Nyokabi's shoulders.

Reaching the privacy of his room, Nyokabi let out a choked sob. Tears welled up in her eyes, spilling over as she spoke in a trembling voice. "Everywhere I look," she lamented, "it seems like Black people are suffering under some form of oppression. Back home, the Kikuyu, Embu, and Meru need a pass just to move around freely in their own country. And here, even after slavery was abolished, people who look like me are still facing oppression."

Devon's heart ached for her. He didn't try to interrupt or offer empty platitudes. Instead, he pulled her close, his arms a silent haven for her grief and frustration. He held her gently, letting her tears flow freely, a silent understanding passing between them.

In that quiet space, words seemed inadequate. Her pain resonated with him; a shared thread of experience woven into the fabric of their connection.

Chapter 37

"You know, I heard that the Africans sold their own as slaves." Devon's mom said at breakfast the next day. "What do you know about that?"

Nyokabi pushes back from the breakfast table, the weight of history settling on her shoulders. "They don't teach us much in school about our own history," she says, her voice thoughtful. "But what I have read paints a complex picture."

She took a deep breath and continued. "Mombasa, our beautiful coastal city, dates back to the 10th century. Even today, the architecture reflects the rich blend of cultures that shaped it. Arabs came to trade, their influence mixing with the Bantu people who already lived there. A touch of Portuguese influence is there too. This melting pot gave birth to the Swahili language and the Swahili people – a vibrant community that still thrives today."

Nyokabi pauses, her eyes scanning the faces around the table. "Most people assume all slaves went to the Americas," she said. "But the truth is, slavery existed in East Africa as well. Arabs, aided by some Africans, fueled a brutal trade in the 19th century. It reached its peak then, devastating vast swathes of the region."

A flicker of mixed emotions crossed her features. "Kenya, thankfully, escaped the worst of it. Our sparse population on the eastern side and the harsh climate made large-scale slave raiding impractical. Caravans heading west often vanished in Maasai territory. Those warriors were fierce protectors."

She smiled faintly and continued. "But the scars are still there. Fort Jesus in Mombasa, built by the Portuguese, became a holding point for captured slaves before they were shipped to Zanzibar, a monstrous market where 120,000 lives were bartered away each year."

Nyokabi's gaze falls, a heavy silence descending upon the table. The sunny breakfast atmosphere had given way to a somber reflection on a dark chapter in history.

The last bites of breakfast disappeared, leaving an empty silence in their wake. Devon's mom, her brow furrowed in contemplation, finally spoke. "Nyokabi," she said, her voice thick with guilt, "your explanation...it challenges everything I thought I knew. Africans selling Africans? It's a truth I never dared to face."

Nyokabi met her gaze, a flicker of sadness crossing her features. "It's a truth that gets buried often," she said softly.

Devon's dad, usually stoic, surprised them all. "You mentioned different treatment for slaves in the East, Nyokabi. Can you tell us more?"

A hint of complexity returned to Nyokabi's expression. "Some slaves in the East might have found themselves working in households, even integrated into families to a certain extent. But make no mistake," she continued, her voice regaining its strength, "the horror still existed. Zanzibar, a major slave market, is a place stained with suffering. The number of souls who died before being sold..." she trailed off, unable to finish the sentence, the thought too painful to bear.

The weight of history hung heavy in the air. This wasn't just breakfast conversation anymore; it was a raw exchange, a peeling back of layers that had been hidden for far too long.

Sensing the need for a moment to breathe, Devon offered a suggestion. "Maybe a break from heavy topics, Nyokabi? Maybe go to the grocery store?"

Nyokabi offered a wan smile, the emotional toll evident. "That sounds lovely, Devon."

Gratitude flickered across Devon's mom's face. "Absolutely! And maybe later," she added, looking at Nyokabi, "you can teach us how to make some of those delicious Kenyan dishes you mentioned?"

A fragile sense of normalcy returned. The conversation had been brutal, and honest, and left them all emotionally raw. But within that rawness, a new seed had been planted - a seed of understanding, of confronting uncomfortable truths together. They were on a journey, not just of love, but of learning, of building bridges across divides, and of ensuring the past wouldn't be buried again. The road ahead wouldn't be easy. There would be more difficult conversations and more challenges. But with each step, their bond would strengthen, their connection deepening, as they navigated the complexities of their multicultural world, hand in hand.

The weight of history hung heavy in the air long after breakfast. Devon helped Nyokabi clear the table, their movements quiet and reflective. As Devon stacked the dishes, a question bubbled up within him.

"Nyokabi," he started hesitantly, "hearing about the slave trade...it made me angry. But also..." he searched for the right words, "confused. Angry at the people who did it, but also...at my own history somehow."

Nyokabi turned, her eyes filled with understanding. "It's a natural reaction, Devon. Slavery tore families apart, and devastated communities. It's a legacy that carries pain for all of us."

They sat down in the living room, a silent connection passing between them. Devon felt a surge of protectiveness towards Nyokabi, a need to share his own burden. "My mom always tried to teach me about Black history, but it was mostly focused on the American experience. This...this fills in a gap I never knew existed."

Nyokabi reached across the table, her touch light on his hand. "We can learn together, Devon," she said softly. "We can explore the stories, the resilience, the fight for freedom that exists in both our heritages."

A spark of determination flickered in Devon's eyes. "Yeah, we can do that." He squeezed her hand gently. "Maybe...maybe we can visit that museum downtown with the African art exhibit. Learn more about the cultures that were stolen away."

Nyokabi smiled. "A wonderful idea. But first," she said, her voice playful, "how about I teach you a few Swahili phrases to impress your friends?"

Their laughter echoed in the kitchen, a light counterpoint to the heaviness of the morning's conversation. Yet, a new understanding thrummed beneath the surface. The legacy of slavery wouldn't disappear, but by facing it together, their love could become a bridge, a testament to the strength and resilience they shared.

Chapter 38

The museum was a bustling hub of history, artifacts whispering stories from across the continent. Devon and Nyokabi wandered through the exhibits, Nyokabi translating the descriptions of intricate masks and vibrant textiles. It was a journey into a shared past, each objects a poignant reminder of the rich tapestry ripped apart by the slave trade.

As they stood before a display of intricately carved wooden figures, a woman with a knowing smile approached them. "Beautiful, aren't they?" she said, her voice warm. "Each one tells a story."

"They are," Nyokabi agreed, her voice filled with pride. "These figures come from the Makonde people of Tanzania. They depict spirits and ancestors."

The woman looked at Devon, a twinkle in her eye. "You must be the young man learning about your roots?"

Devon blushed, a smile tugging at the corner of his lips. "Actually," he said, glancing at Nyokabi, "it's about more than that. We're learning about our heritage together."

The woman's smile widened. "Ah, a love story fueled by history! Wonderful! Do you know about Sankofa, young man?"

Devon shook his head, and Nyokabi leaned in, her gaze curious. The woman explained, "Sankofa is a West African concept. It means 'go back and fetch it.' It's about learning from the past to build a better future."

Devon and Nyokabi exchanged a glance, a silent promise hanging between them. They would learn from the past, honor their ancestors, and build a future where their love story served as a beacon of understanding and unity.

Devon stared out the window, the city lights blurring into a kaleidoscope of colors. The museum visit had been a turning point. Holding Nyokabi's hand as they explored their heritage had woven a new thread of intimacy into their relationship. Now, a different kind of exploration bloomed in his mind - a future with her.

But with that vision came a tangle of worries. Children. The very word sent a tremor of apprehension through him. He loved kids, and always had. But the thought of raising them in a world that still held prejudices, a world where they might be seen as "different," gnawed at him.

He glanced at Nyokabi, lost in a book about Kenyan folktales. Her brow furrowed in concentration, a stray curl escaping her braid. Would she even want children? Had they even discussed it?

Suddenly, insecurity coiled around his throat. He wasn't naive. He'd seen the way some people looked at interracial couples, the subtle shift in their gaze, the microaggressions hidden in casual conversation. Even though they were both black, would their marriage be affected by their different cultures? He couldn't shield his children from that entirely, but the thought of them facing such negativity was a bitter pill to swallow.

Yet, as he watched Nyokabi, a quiet strength emanated from her. He remembered her resilience, the way she spoke about the legacy of slavery with honesty and a fierce pride in her heritage. Maybe, just maybe, their love could create a fortress for their children, a haven built on understanding and acceptance.

He took a deep breath, finally breaking the silence. "Nyokabi," he started hesitantly, "we've been talking about a lot lately...our past, our cultures. Have you ever thought about..." he trailed off, unsure how to phrase the question.

Nyokabi looked up, her eyes warm and inviting. "About a future together, Devon?" she finished gently.

Heat crept up Devon's neck. "Yeah," he admitted. "And kids. Building a family."

Nyokabi smiled, a soft light dancing in her eyes. "It's something I've dreamt of too," she confessed, placing her book down. "But like you, I worry. This world isn't always kind to those who don't fit the mold."

Devon reached for her hand, his fingers intertwining with hers. "Maybe that's why we need to try even harder," he said, his voice gaining conviction. "We can teach our children about both sides of their heritage, instill in them a sense of pride and the courage to stand tall. We can create a world for them, even if it's just within our own home, they will also have roots in Kenya, where love and acceptance are the cornerstones."

Nyokabi squeezed his hand. "Together," she echoed, her voice filled with a quiet determination that mirrored his own. "We face the challenges together, Devon. And who knows, maybe our children, raised with love and understanding, can be a part of changing the world for the better."

A sense of peace settled over Devon. The path wouldn't be easy, but with Nyokabi by his side, he was ready to face the future, whatever it held. Their love story, a tapestry woven from shared history and newfound dreams, had just begun a new chapter.

Chapter 39

Back at college, life settled into a familiar rhythm. Yet everything felt subtly different. Devon carried a newfound purpose in his heart, fueled by his conversations with Nyokabi and the shared strength they discovered at the museum. He dove deeper into his African American history studies, the injustices of the past igniting a fire within him to fight for a more equitable future.

Nyokabi thrived in her classes, her Kenyan heritage becoming a source of pride she readily shared with classmates. They'd attend African student association events, Nyokabi introducing Devon to vibrant drumming circles and delicious potlucks filled with unfamiliar flavors. In return, Devon took her to soul food restaurants and poetry readings, their explorations a delicious blend of cultures.

With each passing day, Devon's desire to solidify his future with Nyokabi intensified. He envisioned lazy mornings with her laughter filling the tiny apartment, evenings spent discussing their dreams, and maybe, someday, a little one with bright eyes.

One crisp autumn afternoon, Devon gathered his courage. He'd meticulously planned a surprise proposal, picturing it under the vibrant foliage of the Howard college grounds. But fate, as it often does, had other plans.

As Nyokabi sat engrossed in a Swahili literature textbook, Devon nervously paced his cluttered dorm room. He fumbled with the velvet box in his pocket, the weight of the ring a tangible symbol of his commitment.

Suddenly, a knock on the door shattered his carefully crafted plan. Nyokabi looked up, a furrow in her brow. "Who could that be?" she wondered, rising to answer.

Devon followed her, his heart pounding an erratic rhythm. He peeked through the crack in the door, his breath catching. Standing on the other side was a tall, imposing figure, his face etched with concern.

"Nyokabi?" the man boomed; his voice thick with a Kenyan accent. Nyokabi's eyes widened in surprise. "Wanjau!" she exclaimed, throwing her arms around the man in a warm embrace.

Devon watched the reunion, a flicker of unease flickering across his chest. Who was this man? And how would his arrival impact his carefully crafted proposal plans?

Chapter 40

The air crackled with tension as Nyokabi's step-brother Wanjau loomed in the doorway. Nyokabi's initial joy morphed into a worried frown. "Wanjau? What are you doing here?"

"There's been trouble, Nyokabi," Wanjau said, his voice grave." Sister Madonna. She's very ill, and things aren't looking good."

Nyokabi's breath hitched. Sister Madonna, was the bedrock of her childhood, a woman who had instilled in her a fierce sense of pride in her abilities. The thought of her being ill was unbearable.

Devon watched the exchange, his heart sinking. This unexpected visit shattered his meticulously planned proposal. More importantly, it threw Nyokabi's world into turmoil.

"When do we leave?" Nyokabi asked, her voice tight.

"Tonight," Wanjau replied, his expression grim. "There's no time to waste. She doesn't have a lot of time left."

The next few hours were a blur of frantic packing and tearful goodbyes. Devon felt helpless, a silent witness to Nyokabi's anguish. He yearned to offer comfort, but the gravity of the situation left little room for romance.

As they hurried to leave for the airport, Nyokabi turned to Devon, her eyes filled with unshed tears. "Devon, I..." she started, her voice choked with emotion.

The crisp autumn air swirled around Nyokabi like a flurry of whispered doubts. Devon stood before her, his face glowing with a nervous excitement. In his hand, a velvet box gleamed, catching the sunlight like a captured rainbow. He proposed, right there under the vibrant foliage of the Howard campus, their love story etched forever in the vibrant tapestry of fallen leaves.

Nyokabi's heart overflowed with a joy so intense it threatened to burst. Yet, intertwined with the euphoria was a knot of worry that tightened with each passing second. The ring on her finger felt like a weight, a symbol of not just their love, but the potential storm it could unleash back in Kenya.

"Devon," she began, her voice a hesitant whisper. "This is..."

He took her hand, his touch grounding her. "The happiest day of my life," he finished, his smile unwavering. "But I know there's more. What's troubling you?"

She met his gaze, the warmth in his eyes battling the fear gnawing at her. "My family, Devon. How will they react to...us?"

Devon's smile softened, a flicker of understanding crossing his face. The issue of different cultures, a hurdle they'd discussed in hushed tones, now loomed large, a potential roadblock on their path.

"I know it won't be easy, Nyokabi," he said, his voice sincere. "But our love is real, and that's what matters. We can face their doubts together."

Nyokabi yearned to believe him, to share the unbridled joy of their engagement. But the image of her father's stern face, his traditional Kenyan values deeply ingrained, flickered in her mind.

"I need to tell them, Devon," she said, her voice resolute. "And soon. But first, I need to be there for them. Wanjau's news..."

She trailed off, the pain of Sister Madonna's condition still raw. Devon squeezed her hand, his eyes reflecting a deep empathy.

"Of course," he said, his voice gentle. "Go home, be with your family. I'll be waiting for you here, waiting for us to face this together."

A wave of gratitude washed over Nyokabi. His unwavering support was a beacon in the storm brewing within her. Leaning in, she planted a soft kiss on his lips, a silent promise hanging between them.

The goodbyes at the airport were bittersweet. Leaving Devon behind felt like leaving a part of her heart, but the journey back to Kenya, once filled with dread, now carried a sliver of hope. Perhaps, armed with love and courage, she could carve a path for their future, a path that bridged the cultural divide and embraced the beauty of their intercultural love story.

Chapter 41

The roar of the engines filled the cabin, a constant hum that mimicked the disquiet in Nyokabi's heart. As the plane soared above the Atlantic, calm fluffy clouds stretched beneath them—a stark contrast to the turmoil brewing within her. The weight of the diamond ring on her finger felt heavier with each passing mile.

Devon's face, etched with a mixture of love and concern, flashed in her mind. His unwavering support was a comfort, but it couldn't erase the apprehension gnawing at her. Back in Kenya, amidst the familiar sights and smells, a different kind of challenge awaited – her family.

She replayed their conversation a hundred times. How would she explain her love for a man whose heritage, vibrant as it was, wasn't woven into the fabric of Kenyan society? Images of her father, a respected elder in their village, his face etched with stoicism, flickered in her mind. His silence at the mention of interracial relationships during their past conversations echoed in her ears.

Doubt, a serpent coiling around her optimism, squeezed tighter. Maybe Devon was right. Maybe their love could conquer all. But a part of her, raised on Kenyan traditions, couldn't ignore the potential storm her announcement could unleash.

She flipped through a magazine, the glossy pages offering a temporary escape. Yet, between the articles on fashion and travel, her mind kept drifting back to Devon. The memory of his proposal, his nervous excitement mirrored by her own overwhelming joy, brought a flicker of warmth to her chest.

Then, a different memory surfaced – Sister Madonna, strong and wise, her eyes twinkling with a mischievous glint whenever Nyokabi spoke to her. "We are stronger than we know." She had said.

A single tear rolled down Nyokabi's cheek. Maybe, just maybe, Sister Madonna's words held a grain of truth. Perhaps, love, like a persistent seed, could take root even in the most unexpected places, challenging traditions and blooming into something beautiful.

With a newfound resolve, Nyokabi wiped away her tears. The journey ahead wouldn't be easy, but she wouldn't face it alone. She had Devon's love in her heart, and Sister Madonna's words ringing in her ears. Taking a deep breath, she straightened her spine, ready to face her family and fight for a future where love, not culture, dictated their happily-ever-after.

Chapter 42

Nyokabi closed her eyes, trying to conjure the image of her childhood home. But the years had blurred the details, leaving only a hazy yearning in her heart. She tried to reach deep into her memories hoping to hear her brother's voice in her head. A vision of her father's face came to mind. As it became clearer a look of worry and love with suppressed tears masked his pain. This was what he looked like when she waved goodbye the day she left for America.

She knew he was longing to see her as much as she longed to see him. She opened her eyes as she smelled her mother's cooking. "It can't be," she murmured as she looked around. She was still on the plane but could still smell the familiar aroma of a home-cooked meal. She turned around and noticed the flight attendants coming down the aisle with food. *Kenya Airways, serving Kenyan cuisine*, she concluded with a smile.

The passenger next to her was looking at her with concern. Nyokabi gave her an embarrassed smile. "Nothing. Just feeling nostalgic" she said as she put her tray down.

As she ate her meal, she thought about her brother who must be taller than her now. He was still a child when she left. She wondered if he still had the same energy and level of activity he had when she last saw him. Before she boarded the plane out of the United States, she had bought a toy car for him. Her brows narrowed. *He is a teenager now! Almost a man! That is not an appropriate gift for him!* she thought. She started biting the inside of her cheeks like she always did when she was nervous. She got up and walked to the bathroom. She did not need to go but she had a lot of nervous energy and needed a short walk. What if they don't like their presents? What if she did not fit in anymore?

I can't wait to see them but I am not sure who they are anymore, she thought. In the bathroom, she looked in the mirror and washed her face. She was thinking about all her life's milestones that her parents did not get to witness. She pulled a letter out of her pocket. It had a stain on it and it was creased in so many areas. She was delicate with it as she unfolded it.

Nyokabi,

I hope you are doing well. We miss you very much and would love to see your face one day soon.

Love,

Mom and Dad.

She read it again. It felt like every time she felt out of sorts, she reached for this letter for reassurance. A sense of calm washed over her. "I miss you too. I am on my way," she whispered as she put it back in her pocket. She walked back to her seat as the flight attendants were walking down the aisle gathering the meal trays. There were two hours left on the flight and she had to try and relax as much as she could.

She pulled the airplane blanket up to her neck and closed her eyes. She immersed herself in the memories of the warmth of the African sun caressing her skin, the sensation of vibrating energy that surrounded her as a child. The song, dance, and the drums made the ground vibrate under her bare feet. She had missed that familiar feeling of love from generations past. There was a palpable energy that embraced her. She smiled she knew that familiar feeling of home. As if the ancestors flew up to the sky to greet her and welcome her home.

She sighed wondering if Devon would be accepted by her family.

"Ladies and gentlemen, we are approaching Jomo Kenyatta international airport, and Kenya Airways welcomes you to Nairobi, Kenya, or better known to many as the capital of Kenya. The local time is 10 am and the temperature is 23 degrees Celsius. To all the passengers who are visiting, we hope you enjoy the beautiful, magical Kenya and to all the Kenyans and residents we say, "Karibuni Nyumbani" (welcome home). It was a pleasure having you on board! Thank you for flying with us."

"Mabibi na mabwana tunakaribia uwanja wa ndege wa Jomo Kenyatta na Shirika la ndege la Kenya la wa karibisha Nairobi. Kwa abiria wote wanaozuru, ni matumaini yetu ya kwamba mta pendezwa na nchi ya Kenya, na kwa wakenya wote, karibuni nyumbani. Kwa niaba ya ndege ya Kenya twa washukuru nyote kwa kuchagua kusafiri nasi, na twawatakia siku njema."

Nyokabi adjusted herself in her seat. She wondered who would be waiting for her at the airport. If no one was at the airport, she would be forced to figure things out by herself. She could always take a taxi but she knew things had changed so much since she was home. She was unsure if she would be able to find the way home with ease. She heard that the newly independent government had simply adopted the colonialist's constitution The thought of returning to an independent

Kenya was great but what did that mean for her family, which had been living in a land reserve.

She wondered if her family was still in the reserve getting food rations and being watched by home-guards. She clenched her fist and her brows creased. *Did the new government need to consult Britain on decisions? Was Kenya still paying taxes to Britain? How was that independence?*

"Are you OK? said the lady sitting next to her on the plane. "You look a little worried."

Nyokabi managed to give the lady a weak smile. She started biting the inside of her cheek again as she thought about Devon and who she had become.

"I am ok. I just haven't been home in a while." Nyokabi responded.

"Why do you look worried?"

"I am going to have to tell my family that I will be getting married soon. The man is not Kikuyu, he is African American."

"Oh! You must be nervous about what they will think about that."

"Among other things"

"Will it be a traditional wedding?"

"I still don't know. He and his family would not know what to do. I guess we have to figure that out."

"I am sure if they are willing to learn, someone will show them what to do."

The lady squeezed Nyokabi's hand which was still clenched. Nyokabi relaxed visibly and smiled.

Nyokabi looked out the window and for the first time in years, she could see her beautiful country. Everything was so green, save for the cracks that carried fresh clean water down the mountains and the picturesque waterfalls. She could have sworn she saw some animals moving on the ground even though at that altitude they would appear to be just dots on the ground. The intensity of the realization of how much she had missed home and all its beauty was overwhelming. Tears were flowing freely down her face and she did not make an effort to hide them.

Wanjau who was sitting behind her watched his step-sister protectively.

Chapter 43

The days that followed stretched into agonizing weeks. Communication with Nyokabi was limited to brief, anxious messages. He learned little about Sister Madonna's condition, only that the situation remained critical.

The vibrant colors of autumn bled into the harsh reality of winter. The once-festive atmosphere on campus now felt hollow. Devon poured his anxieties into his studies, finding solace in the familiar rhythm of lectures and assignments. Yet, his thoughts constantly drifted back to Nyokabi, a constant ache in his chest.

One evening, huddled in his dorm room with a mug of hot cocoa, staring at his luggage, a knock on his dorm room startled him. Someone handed him a piece of paper. A telegram from Nyokabi.

"Devon," the message read. "Sister Madonna passed away peacefully this morning. I'm coming back soon."

Excitement filled his heart. He still had time to go visit his parents for the weekend.

The 5:30 pm flight from Washington DC to Los Angeles felt like an eternity for Devon. Every passing minute stretched into an agonizing hour, the cramped airplane seat offering no solace for the ache in his heart. Nyokabi had been gone for weeks, and the usually vibrant campus of Howard felt like a ghost town without her. He missed their stolen moments of study breaks, the way her laughter could fill even the drabbest lecture hall with warmth, and the quiet comfort of her presence by his side.

Landing in LA felt more like a descent into a different world. The dry heat of California contrasted sharply with the crisp autumn air of Washington DC. He hailed a cab, the familiar sights and sounds of his childhood bringing a wave of nostalgia, but it wasn't enough to dispel the emptiness that clung to him.

At his parent's house, a warm hug from his mom and a playful jab from his dad offered a temporary reprieve. Yet, the familiar routine of weekend dinners and backyard barbecues felt hollow without Nyokabi's bright smile gracing the table. His family, ever perceptive, picked up on his melancholy.

"Still pining after that Kenyan beauty, son?" his dad teased, a twinkle in his eye. Devon couldn't help but chuckle, the memory of Nyokabi's infectious laugh warming him from the inside.

The next evening, as they sat on the porch swing, watching the fiery California sunset paint the sky in vibrant hues, Devon confided in his father. He spoke about his love for Nyokabi, his worries about her family's reaction to their interracial relationship, and the uncertainty that gnawed at him.

His father, a man weathered by time and experience, listened patiently. "Love, son," he said, his voice gruff but gentle, "is a powerful thing. It can bridge oceans and cultures, but it takes courage and understanding. You gotta believe in what you have with Nyokabi, and be willing to fight for it."

Devon felt a surge of warmth spread through him. He realized that while Nyokabi's absence created a void, it couldn't extinguish the flame of their love. This visit home, a reminder of his roots and his family's unwavering support, had also rekindled his determination.

Chapter 44

That night, after Devon's father had gone to work, Devon went to his room and tried to go to sleep. He tucked Nyokabi's picture under his pillow and tried to get comfortable. Devon had been laying down for a while now, staring at the ceiling. His room was dark, but the usual peace was shattered by the garish blue and white lights filtering through his window. They pulsed like a mocking reminder of the chaos unfolding outside. A muffled yell pierced the night, "Stop resisting!"

Devon flinched, his grip tightening on a worn photograph that he was pulling from under his pillow. It was a picture of Nyokabi, her smile as bright as the intrusive lights, her eyes sparkling with warmth. However, she was a world away from the violence erupting outside.

Another yell, "What is going on?' It was a woman's voice laced with raw panic. Devon squeezed his eyes shut, the image of Nyokabi burning brighter in his mind. He could almost hear her infectious laugh, a sound that always chased away his worries. But here, in the face of this relentless violence, even the memory of her laughter felt fragile.

A knock on his bedroom door startled him. "Devon, are you in there?" It was his mom's voice, laced with concern.

"Yes Mom, same old shit going on out there."

"Okay, you better get some sleep and stop worrying about Nyokabi."

Devon knew his mom was trying to be reassuring, but sleep felt like a distant dream. He turned over several times, the image of Nyokabi refusing to be dislodged from his thoughts.

Gunshots rang out, shattering the fragile peace. Devon dove to the floor, a scream piercing the night air. Two more shots punctuated the scream, a horrifying symphony of violence.

"Why!? He did nothing. He was just sitting outside his house!" The woman's voice was raw with grief.

A hollow calm settled over Devon as the scene unfolded down the street. He didn't move, didn't look out the window.

"He tried to reach for my gun," the man who had been yelling commands spoke, his voice now calmer.

Another deep voice yelled back.

"You better get back." he continued in a condescending tone. "Don't come any closer."

Sirens wailed in the distance, a mournful counterpoint to the human drama playing out on the street.

Devon slowly got up and sat on his bed, his gaze fixed on the photo clutched in his hand. He didn't need to look outside to know what he'd see. The image of Nyokabi's vibrant smile felt like a cruel taunt in the face of this relentless reality.

"I think they just killed another black boy," Devon said, his voice barely a whisper.

His mother rushed into the room; her face etched with worry. She pulled him into a hug, her touch a small comfort in the face of the overwhelming fear.

"Did you hear that?" she asked. "Were those gunshots? Lord have mercy! Someone just lost a child!"

She pulled Devon a little closer protectively.

"I think Nyokabi is better off in Kenya," he said. "I don't want to marry her and have her in this environment."

Devon's mother rubbed his back, her voice soothing. "You love each other. You two will figure that out."

But even as she spoke, a seed of doubt had been planted. Devon loved Nyokabi, there was no question about that. But could his love protect her from this relentless violence? Was marrying her condemning her to a life of fear? The weight of these questions pressed down on him, a heavy burden amidst the chaos of the night.

Chapter 45

The brutal encounter on the street left Devon reeling. The image of Nyokabi's vibrant smile, a beacon of hope during his lonely nights, now flickered with a new vulnerability. Fear, a cold serpent, coiled around his heart.

Back at his college dorm, the familiar surroundings offered no solace. Sleep, usually a welcome escape, felt like a distant dream. The echoes of sirens and the woman's raw scream haunted him.

Doubt, a persistent seed planted by the violence, began to sprout. Could his love for Nyokabi truly shield her from the harsh realities of his world? Was bringing her into this environment, where safety seemed like a privilege reserved for some, a selfish act?

These questions gnawed at him, a constant undercurrent to his interactions with friends and studies. He found himself gravitating towards discussions on police brutality and racial injustice, desperately seeking answers. He devoured articles, participated in protests, and channeled his anger into action, searching for a way to make a difference, to create a world where Nyokabi wouldn't have to live in fear.

Yet, amidst the turmoil, one truth remained unwavering – his love for Nyokabi. The letters he received from her, filled with warmth and understanding, were a lifeline. Her belief

NYOKABI

in him, and her willingness to face the challenges together, rekindled his hope.

However, the anger simmered beneath the surface. The incident had ignited a fire within him, a burning desire to create a future where Nyokabi wouldn't have to live in constant fear, where the color of their skin wouldn't be a cause for apprehension. He knew he couldn't change the past, but he could work towards a better tomorrow, and that fight would start with having an honest conversation with Nyokabi.

Devon's frame of mind was a complex mix of love, fear, and determination. He loved Nyokabi fiercely, but the events had forced him to confront the harsh realities of the world they lived in. He was determined to fight for their love, to create a safe haven for them, but the path wouldn't be easy. It would require honest conversations, unwavering support, and a commitment to building a future where love could conquer not just distance, but societal divisions as well.

The silence in his dorm room was deafening. Devon fiddled with a worn photograph of Nyokabi, her smile a stark contrast to the emptiness radiating from the empty armchair opposite him. Weeks had crawled by since her departure for Kenya, and the vibrant colors of autumn seemed muted without her vibrant spirit to share them with.

He wandered aimlessly around the cramped space, their shared textbooks abandoned on the coffee table. He longed for the sound of her gentle laughter, the lilt of her Swahili phrases that always made him smile, even if he didn't quite understand them.

Restlessness gnawed at him. He couldn't just sit around, moping. He grabbed his worn sneakers and headed out, the crisp autumn air offering a welcome change from the stale air of the dorm. He wandered through the streets, past familiar landmarks that now held a bittersweet significance.

He ended up at the Museum, a place they had often visited together. As he walked through the exhibits, the stories of struggle and resilience resonated with him. He felt a surge of pride in his heritage, a wellspring of strength to face his own challenges.

Suddenly, an idea sparked in his mind. Back at the dorm, he rummaged through his dusty box of childhood mementos, finally pulling out a worn leather-bound journal. He started writing, pouring out his thoughts and feelings for Nyokabi. He described their adventures in Washington, shared snippets of conversations they'd had, and recounted his experiences exploring his own African American heritage.

He wrote about his dreams for their future, a future where their cultures intertwined, a tapestry woven from love and understanding. As the hours melted away, he filled countless pages, each word a bridge across the miles, a testament to his love and commitment.

When he finally finished, a sense of peace settled over him. He knew he couldn't control the outcome of her conversation with her family, but he could express his deepest feelings, his unwavering love for her. He sealed the journal with a stamp, a small symbol of the unbreakable bond he felt with Nyokabi.

He wouldn't send it yet. When she returned, he would present it to her in person, a tangible expression of their journey together, a love story waiting to be continued. Until then, he would focus on his studies, draw strength from his heritage, and wait for the day her bright smile would fill their shared space once more. With each passing day, his resolve grew stronger. He wouldn't let distance or cultural differences dim the light of their love. He had his voice, his heart, and a journal filled with promises, a potent arsenal to fight for their future together.

Chapter 46

The weight of grief pressed down on Nyokabi like a tangible force as the plane touched down in Washington DC. The crisp autumn air, once a welcome change from the summer heat, now felt like a slap in the face. The vibrant foliage that had adorned the Howard Campus when she left seemed muted, mirroring the dull ache in her chest.

Weeks in Kenya had been a blur of tearful goodbyes, and comforting rituals. Yet, even amidst the grief, a flicker of hope had bloomed – a hope nurtured by the promise whispered across the miles in Devon's heartfelt letters. Kenya, post-independence was a pleasant surprise as she saw her fellow Kenyans working towards building the country. Kenya was in good hands.

Stepping off the plane, she scanned the crowd of waiting passengers. A familiar figure, his broad shoulders hunched slightly with worry, stood out amidst the throng. As their eyes met, a wave of relief washed over her. He rushed forward, his arms enveloping her in a tight embrace. The scent of his cologne, a comforting reminder of home, filled her senses. Tears welled up in her eyes, but this time, they were tinged with fragile hope.

"Nyokabi," he whispered, his voice thick with emotion. "You're finally back."

She clung to him, the dam of emotions threatening to burst. Back in their cramped room, the familiar surroundings offered a strange sense of comfort. As Devon helped her unpack, a worn photograph of her family slipped from her bag.

"They are beautiful," he said, his voice a low murmur.

Nyokabi nodded, a faint smile gracing her lips. "They want me to be happy, Devon."

He met her gaze, his eyes filled with a quiet intensity. "And are you?"

The question hung in the air, heavy with unspoken emotions. She traced the lines on his palm with her finger. "Not yet," she admitted, her voice soft. "But I know I will be, with you by my side."

Tears welled up in Devon's eyes. He pulled a worn leather-bound journal from his drawer, its cover adorned with a small stamp as a seal. He handed it to her, his gaze filled with love and a hint of nervousness.

"This is for you," he said.

Nyokabi's heart skipped a beat. She recognized the journal – a treasured possession from Devon's childhood. As she opened it, a torrent of emotions flooded her. Pages filled with Devon's familiar handwriting unfolded her story, their story, woven together with his experiences and his unwavering love.

Tears streamed down her cheeks as she read, each word a bridge across the miles, a testament to the depth of his love. The fear of introducing him to her family, the uncertainty gnawing at her, seemed to melt away with every heartfelt entry.

When she finished, she looked up at Devon, her eyes shining with a newfound resolve. "We can face anything, together," she whispered, her voice trembling with emotion.

Devon pulled her close, his heart overflowing with love and relief. The road ahead wouldn't be easy. The conversation about their future, about navigating cultural differences and facing societal disapproval, loomed large. But in that moment, huddled together in their tiny dorm room, they had each other.

Nyokabi, empowered by Devon's unwavering support and the wisdom passed down from her family, knew their love could be a powerful force. They were ready to face her family, navigate the complexities of their cultural divide, and fight for their happily ever after. Their love story, etched in the pages of a shared journal, was a testament to the enduring power of connection, a love that had blossomed amidst grief and separation, now poised to bloom even brighter in the face of new challenges.

Chapter 47

The air crackled with joyous energy as Nyokabi stood in the throngs of cheering families and fellow students. Today wasn't her day to don the black cap and gown, but watching Devon take the stage at Howard University's graduation ceremony filled her with a fierce pride that rivaled her own graduation a year ago.

He looked handsome, a hint of nervous excitement mingling with the confident smile that split his face as he received his diploma.

Later that evening, under the warm glow of fairy lights strung across their tiny D.C. apartment, the air buzzed with celebratory energy. Friends streamed in, bearing gifts and congratulations for Devon. Laughter mingled with the clinking of champagne flutes as Devon reminisced about his tumultuous law school journey – late nights fueled by takeout and dreams of a just legal system. Nyokabi felt the pressure to start preparing for her own journey through law school.

The next morning, humid D.C. air clung to Nyokabi like a second skin as she unpacked boxes in their tiny apartment. Law school textbooks threatened to topple, their intimidating weight a stark reminder of the journey about to begin. A nervous thrill danced in her stomach, a blend of excitement and trepidation. Across the cramped living room, Devon, already sporting a well-worn suit, chuckled at her anxiety.

"Remember when getting a C in Torts felt like the end of the world?" She teased.

Davon frowned at her playfully. "Not helping, fiancé."

Their engagement ring, glinted in the afternoon light. It had been a whirlwind proposal, squeezed in before Nyokabi's departure to Kenya. Grand plans for a fairytale wedding had been shelved, sacrificed at the altar of their demanding schedules. But the ring, a symbol of their unwavering commitment, warmed Nyokabi's heart.

"Speaking of weddings," Devon started, his voice turning serious. He knelt on one knee beside the overflowing box of legal tomes.

Nyokabi's eyes widened. "Devon? What are you—"

"Nyokabi Njogu," he interrupted, his voice filled with an urgency that surprised her. "Law school for you starts next week, and I've just landed a fantastic job at a social justice firm. Before the craziness gets even crazier, will you marry me? Like, right now?"

Nyokabi stared at him, a mixture of amusement and disbelief warring within her. They'd talked about a courthouse wedding, a simple ceremony to solidify their union before the whirlwind of their careers took hold. But "right now"?

"Are you sure you're not just avoiding unpacking?" she teased, a playful smile tugging at her lips.

Devon grinned. "Maybe a little. But mostly, I don't want to start this new chapter without you by my side, as my wife."

A warm wave of emotion washed over Nyokabi. Looking into Devon's eyes, brimming with love and a touch of nervous anticipation, she knew this wasn't just about convenience. It was about facing the unknown, together.

"Yes, Devon," she whispered, tears welling up in her eyes. "A thousand times yes."

Devon beamed, they made their way to the courthouse and got their marriage license. When the day came, Devon slipped the same ring onto her finger. The familiar ring suddenly felt incredibly meaningful, a symbol of their love and their shared commitment to navigate the complexities of life, law school, and their careers, as a team. Their "right now" wedding might not have been the fairytale they'd once envisioned, but it held the promise of a future built on love, support, and a shared passion for justice. The path ahead was uncertain, but they knew they would face it together, husband and wife.

Chapter 48

Nyokabi's law school years flew by like the wind. The crisp May air of Washington D.C. crackled with a nervous energy that mirrored Nyokabi's own. Today wasn't just graduation day; it was the culmination of years of relentless studying, late nights fueled by coffee and ambition, and a shared dream with Devon by her side. As she adjusted her mortarboard and smoothed out the wrinkles of her gown, her gaze swept across the sea of proud faces. There was her brother Wanjau, Sister Marie Claire, and a few friends, beaming with a mix of pride and relief, their eyes glistening with tears. And then there was Devon, his face a portrait of pure joy, a single red rose clutched in his hand.

Later that evening, Devon presented Nyokabi with a new leather-bound journal. "For your next chapter," he said, his voice thick with emotion.

Nyokabi traced the inscription on the cover: "To Nyokabi, the future defender of justice. May your journey be filled with purpose and your heart forever burn with the fire of truth." Tears welled up in her eyes as she looked up at Devon. His own eyes shone with a love that transcended words.

"But there's more," Devon continued, a mischievous glint in his eyes. He produced two plane tickets, and their destination was Nairobi, Kenya.

Nyokabi gasped, a wave of surprise and excitement washing over her. "Devon, you're serious?"

Devon grinned. "Absolutely. It's time I experienced your homeland, the place that made you who you are. Besides," he added, winking, "your parents need to celebrate you and someone needs to be your personal photographer on this victory lap."

The flight to Nairobi was a whirlwind of emotions for Devon. Gazing out the window at the vast expanse of the African continent, a sense of ancestral connection bloomed within him. He devoured every detail— the patchwork of cultivated fields, the meandering rivers, the clusters of traditional mud huts nestled amongst the trees. Landing in Nairobi, a sensory overload awaited – the vibrant cacophony of the marketplace, the heady mix of spices and aromas, the warm smiles and curious glances from passersby.

Nyokabi reveled in introducing Devon to her world, but there was one crucial step before they embarked on adventures: meeting her parents. A hint of nervousness fluttered in her stomach as they approached the familiar, sun-baked brick house in Murang'a.

Her parents greeted them with open arms and wider smiles. For Nyokabi's mother, it was a moment she'd dreamt of – her daughter, the lawyer, returning home with a successful man by her side. Her father, a man of few words, clapped Devon on the shoulder, his gruff demeanor masking a quiet pride.

The following days were a beautiful blend of introductions and cultural immersion. Devon, ever the charmer, attempted (and mostly failed) to master a few Swahili phrases, much to the amusement of Nyokabi's family. They shared stories, meals cooked over open fires, and evenings spent under the starlit sky, the Milky Way stretching like a luminous river above them.

One evening, as they sat around a crackling bonfire, Nyokabi's father turned to Devon, his gaze steady. "We are proud of Nyokabi," he began, his voice low and raspy. "She is strong, intelligent, and fights for what is right. We hope you will treat her well and support her dreams."

Devon met his gaze, his own filled with sincerity. "Nyokabi inspires me every day, sir. I promise to be by her side, always."

A satisfied smile played on Nyokabi's father's lips. He placed a weathered hand on Devon's shoulder, a silent gesture of acceptance. With that simple act, Devon was officially welcomed into the family.

They visited the Convent where she grew up, Sister Maria's kind eyes crinkling with delight at their arrival. Sister Madonna's absence was a palpable heaviness. They explored bustling Nairobi markets, Devon's bargaining skills tested by the quick-witted Kenyan vendors. They embarked on a thrilling safari, the sight of majestic lions and playful elephants etching memories forever in their hearts.

One starlit evening, perched on a scenic overlook with the city lights of Nairobi twinkling below, Devon turned to Nyokabi, his voice filled with awe. "This place is incredible, Nyokabi. The energy, the resilience, the beauty... It's spiritual, it's unlike anything I've ever experienced."

Nyokabi squeezed his hand. "I'm glad you see it, Devon. This is where my passion for justice was born, where I witnessed the struggles of everyday people and the fight for a better life."

Their Kenyan adventure wasn't just a vacation; it was a bridge between their worlds, a shared experience that deepened their love and understanding. As they boarded the plane back to D.C., they carried with them not just souvenirs and photographs, but a renewed sense of purpose and the blessings of Nyokabi's family. Together, they were ready to face the challenges that lay ahead, their love story a testament to the unifying power of shared dreams and a deep connection that transcended borders.

Chapter 49

The scent of freshly brewed coffee and ambition hung heavy in the air as Nyokabi stepped into the opulent lobby of Kensington Law. The prestigious firm gleamed with mahogany paneling and brass accents, a stark contrast to the sun-baked streets of Nairobi she'd left behind just weeks ago. Law school acceptance had been a dream come true, but landing this summer internship felt like a surreal leap into the big leagues.

A figure emerged from behind a towering oak desk. Tall and impeccably dressed, Kai flashed a smile that could disarm a jury. "Nyokabi? Welcome to Kensington. I'm Kai, your mentor for the summer." His voice was smooth as butter, his handshake firm and confident.

Over the next few weeks, Kai became Nyokabi's whirlwind guide to the fast-paced world of corporate law. He possessed an almost uncanny knack for dissecting complex cases and crafting winning strategies. Yet, a nagging unease settled in Nyokabi's gut whenever Kai skirted the edges of ethical practice. He'd dismiss her concerns with a playful wink, "Don't worry, Nyokabi. In this game, everyone bends the rules a little."

One evening, hunched over a mountain of case files, Nyokabi found herself captivated by Kai's effortless charm. He effortlessly weaved jokes into legal discussions, making the long hours fly by. As the city lights twinkled outside their window, their conversation turned personal. He spoke of his admiration for her tenacity and sharp legal mind, his words leaving a warm flutter in her chest.

Chapter 50

The case landed on Nyokabi's desk with a thud. It was a seemingly straightforward breach of contract lawsuit, but a nagging suspicion gnawed at her. Kai, however, saw it as a golden opportunity. "This is a slam dunk, Nyokabi. Just a few tweaks here and there, and we'll have a win that'll boost both our careers."

His "tweaks" involved manipulating evidence and exploiting a technicality in the contract. Nyokabi's conscience screamed, but a part of her craved Kai's approval. Maybe this was just the way the game was played, the necessary evil to succeed in this cutthroat world.

Days turned into weeks, the weight of the secret growing heavier with each passing night. Finally, the pressure became unbearable. Nyokabi cornered Kai in a deserted conference room, her voice trembling as she laid out her concerns. A flicker of surprise crossed his face, replaced by a practiced smile. "Everyone bends the rules, Nyokabi. It's about winning," he said, his voice dismissive.

Disillusionment washed over Nyokabi. This wasn't the legal world she'd envisioned. She stood up, her voice firm despite the tremor in her hands. "I can't be a part of this, Kai." Leaving the room, she felt a strange mix of relief and apprehension.

Chapter 51

Returning to the apartment where she and Devon had spent their college years felt both nostalgic and daunting. Landing the summer internship at Kensington Law had been a dream come true, but the ethical gray areas she'd encountered gnawed at her. Seeing Devon, her rock and confidant, was a much-needed balm.

Their tiny apartment, a haven during their Howard law school days, felt even cozier now. The worn furniture and mismatched mugs held memories of late-night study sessions fueled by takeout and laughter. Devon, ever the supportive husband, enveloped her in a hug. "Welcome home, counselor," he teased, his eyes sparkling with warmth.

Over steaming mugs of Kenyan tea, Nyokabi poured out her heart. She spoke of the brilliant but ethically dubious mentor, Kai, and the case that had pushed her to the brink. As she recounted the pressure to manipulate evidence, Devon's brow furrowed. His face, usually etched with a playful smile, hardened with concern.

"This doesn't sound right, Nyokabi," he said, his voice firm. "You shouldn't have to compromise your integrity to succeed." He reminded her of their long talks in the Yard, fueled by dreams of a legal system that championed justice, not just victory at any cost. His words were a much-needed reminder of her core values.

Chapter 52

The weight of the decision to report Kai settled on Nyokabi's shoulders like a leaden cloak. The case files sat accusingly on her desk, a stark reminder of the ethical tightrope she walked. Each stolen glance at Kai, with his practiced smile and unwavering confidence, sent a shiver down her spine. Was this the reality of corporate law? Did winning truly require sacrificing your morals?

The next evening, after a particularly grueling day of research, Nyokabi found solace in a familiar haunt, a cozy Ethiopian restaurant they frequented during their Howard days. The aroma of spices and simmering stews brought back memories of late-night discussions about social justice and their shared dream of making a difference. Looking across the table at Devon, his eyes filled with unwavering support, she knew she couldn't let the dream die.

Chapter 53

The decision gnawed at Nyokabi, a constant itch she couldn't scratch. Finally, she knew she couldn't stay silent. Taking a deep breath, she drafted a letter to Mr. Kensington, the firm's managing partner. Her fingers trembled as she typed, outlining Kai's tactics and her own discomfort with the case. Pulling it out of the typewriter, a wave of anxiety washed over her. It would be on Mr. Kensington's desk first thing in the morning.

The next morning, the tension in the air crackled with anticipation. Nyokabi stole glances at Kai, his face an unreadable mask. Finally, a summons arrived from Mr. Kensington's office. Her heart hammered against her ribs as she entered the opulent space.

Mr. Kensington, a man whose gaze could curdle milk, sat behind a mahogany desk. He listened to her explanation with an impassive air, the silence stretching into an eternity. Finally, he spoke, his voice a low rumble. "We value integrity at Kensington, Ms. Thompson," he said, his words leaving her uncertain. "However, achieving results can sometimes require... creative solutions."

Disappointment washed over Nyokabi. Was this it? Was there no place for her brand of justice in this cutthroat world? Leaving the office, she felt a familiar knot of indecision tighten in her stomach. Report Kai and risk jeopardizing her career, or become complicit in his unethical ways?

Meanwhile, in his office, Devon thought of Nyokabi and was concerned about her. She had poured out her frustrations, the weight of the decision threatening to crush her. Devon, ever her anchor, had tried what he could to support her but he worried about her. He picked up the phone and called her as if on queue.

"You have a choice, Nyokabi," he said, his voice steady. "Don't let anyone take away your values. Remember why you started this journey in the first place."

His words struck a chord deep within her. This wasn't just about the case; it was about the lawyer she wanted to be.

Chapter 54

Anxiety gnawed at Nyokabi like a ravenous beast. Devon's voice, though comforting over the phone, couldn't quell the storm raging within her. Mr. Kensington's words echoed in her mind: "creative solutions."

Was this the price of success in corporate law?

The weight of the decision became unbearable. Images of her younger self, idealistic and passionate about justice during their Howard days, flashed before her eyes. No, she wouldn't become complicit in this. Taking a deep breath, Nyokabi made a decision. She wouldn't bend. She would blow the whistle.

The next morning, the sterile walls of the law firm felt suffocating. Ignoring Kai's surprised stare, Nyokabi marched towards the office of the firm's ethics committee. Her hands trembled as she knocked. Someone said, "Come in."

A panel of three lawyers, their faces etched with a mixture of curiosity and skepticism, greeted her. With a pounding heart, Nyokabi laid bare Kai's unethical tactics and the pressure she faced to manipulate evidence. She presented the incriminating documents, her voice gaining strength with every word.

The committee listened intently; their expressions unreadable. The air grew thick with tension as Nyokabi finished her statement. A long silence followed, broken only by the soft tick of a grandfather clock.

"Thank you, Ms. Thompson," a woman on the committee finally spoke, her voice laced with concern. "We will take your allegations very seriously and conduct a thorough investigation."

Leaving the office, Nyokabi felt a wave of both relief and trepidation. The die was cast. She had exposed the truth, but the consequences remained uncertain. Would they believe her? Would she lose her internship? More importantly, would she ever find a place in the legal world where integrity wasn't a sacrifice but a core value?

Back at her desk, she reached for her phone, dialing Devon's number. His voice, warm and steady, washed over her anxieties. He listened patiently as she recounted the events of the day, his unwavering support a beacon in the storm.

"You did the right thing, Nyokabi," he said, his voice firm. "Even if it's tough now, you'll never regret standing up for what you believe in."

His words offered a much-needed comfort, but the future remained shrouded in uncertainty. Nyokabi knew the investigation could take days, weeks, maybe even longer. The only thing she could do was wait, hoping her whistle would spark change, not just at Kensington Law, but within herself. This wasn't just about winning a case; it was about becoming the lawyer she always envisioned, one who fought for justice, not just victory.

Chapter 55

Days bled into weeks. The silence from Kensington Law was deafening. Nyokabi found herself relegated to photocopying mundane documents, a stark contrast to the high-profile case she'd been assigned to. Kai avoided her gaze, his charm replaced by a frosty silence.

One afternoon, a summons arrived from the ethics committee. Her heart hammered against her ribs as she entered the same sterile office, the same panel of lawyers awaiting her. This time, however, their expressions were unreadable masks.

The lead attorney, a woman with a piercing gaze, spoke first. "Ms. Thompson, after a thorough investigation, we've found evidence to corroborate your claims regarding Mr. Miller's conduct."

A wave of relief washed over Nyokabi. They believed her.

"However," the attorney continued, her voice turning stern, "the committee has decided to handle this matter internally. Mr. Miller will receive a formal reprimand and additional training."

Disappointment clawed at Nyokabi. Was that all? No public censure, no dismissal? It felt like a slap in the wrist, a message that winning still trumped ethics at Kensington Law.

Chapter 56

The news from the ethics committee hit Nyokabi like a punch to the gut. Internal reprimand? That was it? They were willing to overlook unethical behavior in the name of profit. Her voice trembled as she thanked the committee, a bitter taste lingering in her mouth.

Back at her desk, staring at the mountain of meaningless paperwork, a cold fury settled over her. This wasn't the future she'd envisioned. She wouldn't be a cog in a machine that prioritized profit over justice.

With a newfound resolve, Nyokabi marched towards Mr. Kensington's office. His booming voice echoed, "Come in," but the confidence that usually accompanied her steps had vanished. Taking a deep breath, she straightened her spine and entered.

Mr. Kensington, impeccably dressed as always, looked up from his paperwork, a surprised frown creasing his brow. "Ms. Thompson? Is everything alright?"

"No, sir, it's not," Nyokabi replied, her voice surprisingly steady. She laid bare her disappointment with the committee's decision, and the sense of betrayal she felt at the firm's priorities.

"This isn't who I am, Mr. Kensington," she concluded, her voice ringing with conviction. "I can't be a part of a system that disregards ethical codes."

Mr. Kensington listened intently; his expression unreadable. Several tense moments passed before he finally spoke. "I understand your frustration, Ms. Thompson. However, the legal world is a complex one. Sometimes, difficult decisions need to be made."

Nyokabi shook her head. "There are lines that shouldn't be crossed, Mr. Kensington. And I refuse to cross them."

With a deep breath, she placed her resignation letter on his desk. The weight of the decision settled on her shoulders, but it was mixed with a strange sense of liberation. She was walking away, not from her dreams, but from a path that no longer aligned with her values.

Later that day, a box filled with her belongings sat by the door. A pang of sadness flickered at the thought of leaving behind, a possibly lucrative career. As she stepped out into the bustling streets, the uncertainty of the future stretched before her.

Yet, there was a spark in her eyes, a renewed sense of purpose. She might not have conquered corporate law, but she had conquered something far more important—her own integrity. With a determined stride, Nyokabi walked into the unknown, ready to find a place where justice was more than just a word, but the guiding principle of her legal career.

Chapter 57

Back in their apartment, Nyokabi sank onto the worn sofa, the weight of her decision settling on her shoulders. Leaving Kensington Law felt like a defeat, a step backward. Just then, a knock on the door startled her. Devon was still at work, and she wasn't expecting any visitors. Wiping her eyes, she trudged towards the door, her heart heavy.

Opening the door, she was greeted by the sight of a weathered face framed by a white wimple. A gasp escaped her lips. "Sister Maria?"

The elderly nun, her once vibrant eyes crinkled with a warm smile. "Nyokabi, my dear! It's wonderful to see you all grown up."

Sister Maria, her former teacher from Kenya, had become a pillar of strength and guidance in Nyokabi's childhood. Months had passed since they last saw each other, but the connection remained.

"Sister Maria, what are you doing here?" Nyokabi ushered her in, a wave of emotions washing over her.

Sister Maria settled into the armchair, her gaze sweeping across the modest apartment. "I was visiting Sister Marie Claire and had to see you. I also heard the news," she said gently, her voice laced with concern. "About you leaving the internship."

News travel fast! She thought. Nyokabi braced herself, expecting disappointment. Instead, Sister Maria took her hand, her touch warm and comforting. "You did the right thing, child. True success lies not in wealth or prestige, but in staying true to your values."

A tear trickled down Nyokabi's cheek. "But what if I made a mistake? What if I can't find a place where I can fight for justice without compromising my integrity?"

Sister Maria chuckled; a sound as familiar as the hymns they used to sing in the convent. "From the little firecracker you were, Nyokabi, I have no doubt you'll find your path. Remember, the strongest flames often start from the smallest sparks."

From her pocket, Sister Maria produced an envelope. "This arrived for you. The mailman was delivering it when I was walking up to the door."

Nyokabi carefully opened the envelope, her heart pounding in her chest. Inside was a letter, the crisp stationery was adorned with the official seal of a local law firm. Her breath hitched as she scanned the first line: "Dear Ms. Thompson, We are pleased to offer you a position as a ..."

Tears welled up in her eyes as she devoured the letter. It was a chance to work alongside experienced lawyers, fighting for underserved communities in D.C. It wasn't the high-profile career she'd envisioned, but it was a start, a way to use her legal skills for the greater good.

Looking up, she met Sister Maria's gaze, a silent thank you hanging between them.

The nun squeezed her hand. "Never lose sight of the fire within you, Nyokabi. The world needs more young hearts like yours, burning bright with justice."

As Sister Maria departed, her words resonated deeply within Nyokabi. Leaving Kensington Law might have felt like a defeat, but it had also opened a new door. With a newfound sense of purpose and the unwavering support of her loved ones, Nyokabi was ready to embark on the next chapter of her journey, a journey fueled by her passion for justice and the spark ignited by a wise old nun who believed in the power of a young girl's dreams.

Chapter 58

As the dust settled from the Kensington Law debacle, Nyokabi felt a curious calm wash over her. The weight of expectation, the pressure to conform, had lifted. Now, a new vision began to take shape. One rainy afternoon, curled up with a steaming mug of Kenyan tea, she stumbled upon a documentary about the Black Panther Party.

Devon, home for the weekend after a grueling week at his social justice firm, watched beside her, captivated by the passionate speeches and unwavering commitment to justice for marginalized communities. The documentary sparked a conversation, a shared dream that had simmered beneath the surface during their law school days.

"Imagine," Nyokabi said, her voice filled with excitement, "a law firm dedicated to fighting for those who have no voice, for those who can't afford exorbitant legal fees."

Devon's eyes gleamed. "The Panthers need a legal arm, the People's Law Office. It will provide legal aid and fight against police brutality. We can move back to L.A. and be close to my family!"

The idea took root, growing stronger with every discussion. They envisioned a firm that combined their legal expertise with a community focus, one that echoed the ideals of the Black Panther Party but catered to the specific needs of their own diverse communities, a blend of American social justice principles.

There were challenges, of course. Securing funding, building a client base, the sheer logistics of starting their own firm seemed daunting. But as they delved deeper into the possibilities, excitement overshadowed fear. They could leverage Devon's experience at his current firm, his network of contacts, and Nyokabi's research skills honed at Kensington Law. More importantly, they shared a fierce passion for justice.

Late into the night, they brainstormed names, mission statements, and long-term goals. The dream they'd once pushed aside, overshadowed by the pursuit of prestigious internships and high-paying corporate jobs, was reborn. This time, it felt more tangible, more real.

The following weeks were a whirlwind of action. Devon discreetly started reaching out to former colleagues who shared their vision, and potential investors passionate about social justice causes. Nyokabi contacted legal aid organizations in underserved communities, gauging needs and potential partnerships. Their tiny apartment became a temporary office, overflowing with legal briefs, business plans, and takeout containers fueled by late-night brainstorming sessions.

The road ahead wouldn't be easy. They were two young lawyers, venturing out on their own against established firms. But they had each other, a shared passion, and an unwavering belief in the power of law to create positive change. Their journey, inspired by the legacy of the Black Panther Party, wouldn't be about accumulating wealth or prestige. It would be about building a legacy of their own, a legacy of fighting for the voiceless, one case at a time.

Chapter 59

Standing on the balcony of their L.A. apartment, Nyokabi cradled her gently rounded belly, the city lights twinkling below like a promise for the future. A faint scar on her wrist, a remnant of a childhood injury in Kenya, served as a poignant reminder of the journey that led her here. The path hadn't been easy, but it had been worth it.

She had found her voice, her purpose. Beside her, Devon squeezed her hand, his silent support a constant source of strength. The dream of a law firm, a beacon of justice, still flickered in their hearts. But the road to that dream proved steeper than they anticipated.

Securing funding was their first hurdle. Investors, while impressed by their passion, were hesitant to back two unestablished lawyers with a niche focus on social justice. Building a client base in underserved communities proved to be another challenge. Many residents, used to predatory legal practices, were wary of their intentions. The long hours spent building trust, attending community meetings, and offering pro bono consultations began to take their toll.

One evening, exhausted after a particularly draining day, Nyokabi slumped onto the sofa, a wave of doubt washing over her. "Maybe we were too hasty," she confessed, tears welling up in her eyes. "Maybe the dream has to wait."

Devon pulled her close, his voice a steady comfort. "We'll get there, Nyokabi. It just might take a little longer than we thought." He pointed to her stomach. "We have a little one on the way now. That just adds to our reasons to fight, to build a better world for them to grow up in."

His words rekindled a spark within her. They may not have had a fancy office or a team of associates, but they had each other, their unwavering commitment, and a growing community slowly beginning to trust them. They started small, taking on eviction cases, fighting against unfair wage practices, and offering legal guidance on immigration issues. The victories were modest, but the impact was undeniable. A family saved from eviction, a worker receiving their rightful wages – these small wins fueled their determination.

News of their dedication spread slowly but surely. A local non-profit offered them office space in exchange for pro bono legal aid. Law students, inspired by their work, volunteered their time. Slowly, a network of support began to form around them.

The day their first paying client walked through their door, a single mother facing a child custody battle, was a momentous occasion. The cramped office, once a source of discouragement, now felt like a war room, a place where they strategized and fought for those who couldn't afford high-powered legal representation.

Their journey towards a full-fledged law firm was far from over. Challenges remained fundraising woes, long hours, and the ever-present threat of burnout. But as Nyokabi stood on the balcony, the weight of their tiny miracle shifting comfortably within her, she knew they were on the right path.

They had built a foundation, not just for a law firm, but for a life dedicated to justice, a life that would leave a positive mark on their community, and maybe, someday, on the world. The dream, once distant, now felt tangible, a testament to their unwavering spirit and the power of love, purpose, and a whole lot of late nights.

The young girl who once felt out of place, falling in love with a Mau Mau fighter and watching him die, had found a home in the United States with Devon and in a career that was promising to be fulfilling. Love, in the form of Devon, a strong, supportive partner who believed in her dreams as fiercely as she did. And purpose, in the burgeoning law practice they were building together, a beacon of justice for the underserved communities.

The path hadn't been easy. The scars of losing Githinji, a constant reminder of the brutality she'd witnessed, were etched not just on her heart, and wrist, but on her very soul. Leaving Kenya, leaving behind the ghosts of her past, had been a leap of faith, fueled by a yearning for education as a weapon against oppression.

Washington D.C. had been a whirlwind – the culture shock, law school and all its challenges. It had also been the place where she met Devon, a kindred spirit who shared her passion for justice. Together, they'd weathered the storms – the sting of rejection from potential investors, the long nights fueled by quick meals and flickering hope, the exhaustion that threatened to dim their fire, not to mention Kensington Law, the disillusionment that led her to walk away. But here they were still going strong.

NYOKABI

As Devon pulled her closer on the balcony, his arm snaking around her waist, a warmth spread through her. He pressed a kiss to her forehead, his touch a silent reassurance. "Ready for bed, Mama Amani?" he whispered, his voice laced with a tenderness that melted her heart.

Nyokabi leaned into him, a wave of contentment washing over her. "Almost," she murmured, turning her gaze back to the cityscape. The future stretched before them, uncertain yet brimming with possibility. They might not have a sprawling law firm yet, but they had each other, a growing family, and the unwavering belief in the power of justice. And that, Nyokabi knew, was a foundation strong enough to build anything they set their minds to. "So long Githinji." She whispered.

Epilogue

Years later, the sun beat down on a bustling storefront in D.C.'s vibrant Shaw neighborhood. A hand-painted sign in bold lettering proclaimed: "Thompson & Thompson Law Firm - Justice for All." Inside, the once-cramped office had blossomed into a hive of activity. Legal files lined the shelves, sunlight streamed through the windows, and the sounds of animated conversations filled the air.

At her desk, Nyokabi, now a seasoned lawyer with a hint of silver at her temples, reviewed a case file. Her belly, once a constant reminder of their growing family, was now flat again, the memory of their son Jomo's rambunctious toddler years a source of amusement and fond exasperation.

Amani, their firstborn, a spitting image of Nyokabi with her mother's fierce spirit and a twinkle of mischief in her eyes, sat perched on a nearby stool, nose buried in a law book. At fourteen, she was already a passionate advocate for social justice, fueled by bedtime stories of her parents' struggles and dreams.

Jomo, a whirlwind of energy at eight years old, burst into the office, a triumphant grin plastered on his face. "Mama! Mama! I won first place in the school debate!"

Nyokabi scooped him into a hug, her heart swelling with pride. "Amazing job, Jomo! What was the topic?"

"Equal rights for everyone!" Jomo declared, his voice ringing with enthusiasm.

A soft chuckle escaped Devon's lips as he entered the room, a stack of files in his arms. The years had etched a few lines on his face, but his eyes still held the same unwavering love and support for Nyokabi.

"Sounds like someone's been learning a thing or two from his parents," he said, rubbing Jomo's head.

Over the past decade, their small law firm had become a beacon of hope for the underserved community. They had fought countless cases, securing fair wages for exploited workers, preventing wrongful evictions, and giving a voice to the voiceless.

Their success had also brought recognition. Awards lined the shelves of their office, testaments to their dedication. Yet, the most rewarding moments were the quiet victories – the relieved smile of a client finally back on their feet, the glimmer of hope in the eyes of a child facing an uncertain future.

As they stood together, a family united by love and purpose, Nyokabi knew their journey was far from over. The fight for justice was a constant struggle, but they were in it for the long haul. With Amani's growing idealism, Jomo's boundless energy, and Devon's unwavering support by her side, Nyokabi looked towards the future with a fierce determination. The dream they'd nurtured in that cramped apartment all those years ago had blossomed into a reality, a testament to the enduring power of love, resilience, and the unwavering pursuit of a better world.

Real Events In Book.

Back then, initiation ceremonies to mark the end of childhood were festivals that lasted months. The Agikuyu lived in family units (mbari or nyomba) – these family units are descendants of the nine Gikuyu daughters. Everyone belongs to one of the nine clans. Ultimately, all the nine clans form the Gikuyu Nation. (Rurere Rwa Mbari ya Gikuyu). Their unity was further solidified by age-groups (Riika).

At a certain time, thousands of Agikuyu boys and girls went through the initiation process which marked the end of their childhood. Those initiated at the same time became members of the same age group (riika). All the members of a riika had a strong sense of brotherhood and sisterhood. If, however, at a later date, one wished to join an older age group, they would have to slaughter a goat as payment or passage to move up an age-set. These strong bonds helped different age-sets work harmoniously in fulfilling their responsibilities—political, religious and even social.

Also true are the Mau Mau fighters, all description regarding the Agikuyu customs, and some information about slave trade in the coastal region of Kenya and Zanzibar.

Grandpa's Story

Grandpa worked for the East African Standard Newspaper in Nairobi. In 1951, he went on leave without issue, as the state of emergency hadn't been declared yet. The second time he wanted to visit his family in the reserve in 1952, he had to be escorted by the police, for his own protection from the Mau Mau. He was holding his pass the whole time.

Colonial Rule

All references to colonial rule and the placement of Africans are accurate and can be verified in the Kenya National Archives, including Mrs. Cook's letter and rations portions. The Lari Massacre was a real event.

Grandma's Story

My Grandma's name was Wangui. As a child, I heard my Grandma Wangui and her sister recounting stories of how their mother used to hide them under sacks of grain or sugar during the Mau Mau uprising.

Acknowledgements

The journey of completing this novel has been a long and rewarding one, spanning many years. I would like to extend my deepest gratitude to everyone who has supported me along the way.

To my family, your unwavering support and encouragement have been the backbone of my creativity. Thank you for believing in me and giving me the strength to follow my dreams.

To my friends, thank you for your endless inspiration and for always being there to listen, critique, and celebrate each milestone. Your friendship has been a wellspring of motivation.

To my editor George White, your keen eye and insightful suggestions have truly transformed this manuscript. Your dedication and expertise have pushed me to improve and refine every page.

To my beta readers, your feedback has been invaluable. Thank you for your honesty and for helping me see my work through fresh eyes.

Special thanks to the Kenya National Archives for being an incredible resource. The wealth of information I found there was invaluable.

I am deeply inspired by Jomo Kenyatta's "Facing Mt. Kenya," which provided many cultural references that enriched this story.

Above all, a heartfelt tribute to my grandmother, Grace Wangui—please continue resting with the angels. I am honored to be named after you and to have incorporated some of your wonderful stories into this novel.

To my grandfather, Boniface Gichuhi, you continue to be a strong driving force in my life. I am grateful for your unwavering support and for allowing me to use your stories. Your wisdom and experiences have been a cornerstone of this book.

Lastly, to my readers, thank you for taking this journey with me. Your enthusiasm and support mean everything, and I hope this story resonates with you as much as it did with me while writing it.

About Author

Many people have asked about my author journey and how I started. My journey is rooted deeply in my personal experiences and a quest for understanding.

I lived in South Korea for three years after leaving Kenya for the first time. It was during this period that I experienced racism in a very overt and harsh manner for the first time. This wasn't subtle discrimination; it was blatant and distressing. During my time there, I also encountered African American soldiers stationed in South Korea and listened to their experiences as Black people living in the United States, which further fueled my curiosity and concern.

These interactions and experiences left a profound impact on me. I became determined to understand the root cause of such deep-seated hatred towards Black people across various societies. I decided to cancel my multi-entry visa and return to Kenya, my homeland. There, I immersed myself in extensive research, spending countless hours at the Kenya National Archives, sifting through pages of historical documents and records.

My goal was to uncover the origins and reasons behind this pervasive racial animosity. Despite amassing a wealth of information, I found that the answers to my questions remained elusive. However, the vast amount of research I had collected presented an opportunity—I realized that I could channel this information into something constructive.

One day, the idea struck me: why not compile my findings and experiences into a book? This notion of writing was entirely new to me; I had never considered myself a writer. Yet, the desire to share this knowledge and provoke thought in others was powerful.

What began as a quest for personal understanding turned into an 18-year journey of writing my first book. This long process was both challenging and rewarding, ultimately leading to the creation of two additional books.

Through my writings, I hope to shed light on complex issues surrounding race and to foster a sense of empathy and awareness among readers. It has been a long, arduous journey, but seeing my work in the hands of readers makes every moment worthwhile. Thank you for joining me on this journey, and I hope you all enjoy reading my books as much as I did writing them.

Don't miss out!

Visit the website below and you can sign up to receive emails whenever Wangui Turner publishes a new book. There's no charge and no obligation.

https://books2read.com/r/B-A-HWIQB-XVDOD

BOOKS 2 READ

Connecting independent readers to independent writers.

About the Author

Name: Wangui Turner
Genre: Historical fiction
Bio:
Shaped by family stories of resilience in Kenya - Grandma's survival of the Mau Mau, Grandpa's journalist view of colonialism - I write to bridge divides and explore history's impact on everyday lives.

Read more at https://www.wanguiturner.com/.

Milton Keynes UK
Ingram Content Group UK Ltd.
UKHW040837160724
445389UK00001B/28